DIFFICULT PEOPLE

NIGHTWOOD EDITIONS
2018

DIFFICULT PEOPLE

STORIES

BY CATRIONA WRIGHT

Nightwood Editions
P.O. Box 1779
Gibsons, BC VON 1V0
Canada
www.nightwoodeditions.com

EDITOR: Amber McMillan
COVER DESIGN: Emma Dolan
TYPOGRAPHY: Carleton Wilson

 Canada Council **Conseil des Arts**
for the Arts **du Canada**

 BRITISH COLUMBIA
ARTS COUNCIL
An agency of the Province of British Columbia

Nightwood Editions acknowledges the support of the Canada Council for the Arts, which last year invested $153 million to bring the arts to Canadians throughout the country. We also gratefully acknowledge financial support from the Government of Canada and from the Province of British Columbia through the BC Arts Council and the Book Publishing Tax Credit.

This book has been produced on 100% post-consumer recycled, ancient-forest-free paper, processed chlorine-free and printed with vegetable-based dyes.

Printed and bound in Canada.

CIP data available from Library and Archives Canada.

ISBN 978-0-88971-339-0

CONTENTS

CONTENT MODERATOR

A toy airplane crammed between open legs, pale blue wings resting against pink labia. A dirty terrier whimpering while boots stomp and kick, and off-screen teenagers laugh. A dick, a bigger, veinier dick. An ornate swastika tattooed on a flabby back. A beautiful woman with immaculate eye makeup of swirling aubergine and charcoal shadows, wearing a tight black dress, both arms lifted, revealing lustrous auburn armpit hair. A pool of blood, maroon and shining. Two girls, at most thirteen, expressions blurred with alcohol or drugs, flashing a group of cheering men. A cockroach artfully splayed on a pillow. Another girl, even younger, eyes puffy and swollen with tears, holding a broken vodka bottle to her neck. A man, hooded in black and on his knees with another man behind him, screaming and gesturing with a rusted machete.

Clicking and clicking, I deleted most of the customer-reported images and videos, allowing the armpit hair and the cockroach to stay. I glanced at the clock. Break time. I closed my eyes and tried to separate myself from the chaos on the monitor. I imagined blasting the images from my brain before they had a chance to set down roots. I imagined plucking out my eyeballs and soaking them in a vat of antiseptic.

Opening my eyes, I nodded at my supervisor, who nodded back, tapping her watch as a warning not to exceed my time. I walked down a long aisle between other content moderators clicking and clicking, sighing and wincing, clicking and clicking, shaking their heads and chuckling, clicking and clicking, mumbling and chugging spiked energy drinks. Zoe wasn't in her seat, probably off on one of her many breaks. She took more breaks than anyone, at least seven a day, and in my darker moments, I suspected she was pleasuring the supervisor for favours.

The fluorescent lights hummed. The air conditioner whined. In the corner stood a ping pong table in pristine condition, and there were three plump bean bag chairs huddled around a flat screen television, the company's sad attempt at creating an inviting, homey atmosphere. As if anything could make us want to hang out here more than we had to. Everyone escaped the building on their breaks and we all maintained sterile work areas with no pictures of spouses or kids, no *Cathy* cartoons or succulents. We feared a porous border, this soiled universe seeping into our own.

Before I could stomach my egg salad sandwich and orange, I took a short walk outside, through the strip mall landscape whose blandness would, I hoped, soften the impact of a morning spent ensuring the customers who used our app were sheltered from the bestiality, child pornography, gore, filth and infinite misery that swarmed in from all over the globe. Why hadn't Zoe warned me before I started? Why hadn't she said anything before I saw my first beheading?

This job doesn't appear on career aptitude tests or in teenage diaries. It's nobody's first choice. My first choice was English professor. After a childhood of feeling acutely alone, my only escape the many hours I spent at the local library reading novels about magical orphans dying of tuberculosis, I'd considered it my calling to swap literary insights with other people like me.

I was deluded.

Ph.D. in hand, I could only find poverty-wage work as a contract composition instructor chastising first-year students for comma splices, and when my class sizes doubled, then tripled, and when I stopped being able to discern an A paper from a fail, and when one pint after work every day became six, and when I showed up to class thirty minutes late after a morning spent rubbing antibiotic ointment on self-inflicted cigarette burns, I was called into the program director's spacious and sunlit office.

"Do you know why you're here?" she asked, misting her aloe vera plant, an enormous green crown.

"A tenure-track position in Canadian literature became available?" I said hopefully.

She handed me a pile of student evaluations. "She seems hammered all the time," read one. "Her grading is totally random," another. "She should try to dress more professionally, like pencil skirts and lipstick." Someone had drawn a caricature of me as a bespectacled devil radiating stink squiggles and piercing a student with a pitchfork.

"At least I look skinny," I said.

I left that afternoon, the student's portrait my only memento.

The next two months were pizza and YouTube videos of cats careening around on Roombas or tumbling down slides, a fugue state broken only when I received an angry email from my landlord demanding rent. My credit cards were maxed out and my parents—recently retired and still disappointed in my lack of employment, perceived as my giving up on academia—didn't have the means or desire to support me. I needed a job. I fiddled with my resumé, changing the font from Times New Roman to Garamond, then back again. Eventually I landed some interviews at temp agencies.

"We'll call you," a human resources manager named Barbara or Brian would say, shaking my hand, and then I would spend the next week with my phone on my pillow or in my pocket, the ringtone turned up as high as it would go. I would ask my parents and friends to dial my number, just to be sure my phone wasn't broken.

Then, on a particularly low day, I received a Facebook message from Zoe, a high school friend. Even though I hadn't spoken to her in over a decade, I still knew a lot about her because we followed each other on social media. For example, I knew she was recently divorced and had a two-year-old son named Aiden. I knew she drank green smoothies and favoured yoga pants with celestial or geometric prints. I found it strange that she'd contacted me after all these years, but I had fond memories of our time on the swim team together and I assumed she was in need of a friend. It's difficult to meet new people as an adult. I agreed to have coffee with her at a place near my apartment.

Zoe, in sweatshirt and intergalactic leggings, greeted me warmly, though it seemed to take great effort. She ordered two extra shots in her latte. Jumpy and frazzled, she bore no resemblance to the girl I remembered as bright, witty and fierce, a girl who guzzled Southern Comfort and dared all the boys to arm-wrestle. She looked exhausted, almost haggard, with jutting cheekbones and pronounced bags under her eyes. She spoke in wistful jags and digressions about our mutual friends, often forgetting people's names or ending stories abruptly, which at the time I attributed to new motherhood. Her dishevelment charmed me and made me trust her more, relieved she wasn't the healthful, optimistic dynamo she played on social media.

"I heard you might be looking for work," she said.

"Yes," I said. "The academy, the economy, you know how it is..." I blathered self-consciously, unable to overcome the suspicion that my inability to secure a tenure-track job somehow indicated a profound moral failing rather than circumstances beyond my control.

"I might have something for you at my work."

"Really?" I said, taking a long sip of my drink in a bid to suppress my eagerness.

"It's tiring," she said pensively. "But the pay is great and the people are wonderful."

When she spoke, she avoided eye contact, which I assumed was because she knew I had a Ph.D. and was embarrassed to suggest something that didn't align with my higher self, unaware that I had already given up.

"It can't be worse than reading the same paper three hundred times." By *tiring*, I thought Zoe just meant dull, repetitive.

"Right," she said, laughing too loud and for too long. "So you're ready then?"

Later that week, Zoe prepped me for the interview with strict and exacting instructions: "Describe a time you felt pressured at work," Zoe asked in interviewer mode, her posture suddenly impeccable.

"What exactly will I be doing?" I asked. When she'd first told me about the job, I'd gotten the impression it was more or less guaranteed as long as she gave a recommendation, so this role-playing struck me as redundant and potentially demeaning. It turned out I still had some residual pride.

"Data management, data entry, cataloguing images, archiving," Zoe said, flustered, her voice raised. "Are you going to take this seriously or not?"

I suspected there was more to it than that, but I didn't want to push her, not when she was so clearly aggravated and when I so clearly needed employment. Besides, I knew how hard it could be to describe your work to someone else when you knew so much and your interlocutor so little. I'd spent years in a dusty carrel enraptured with my thesis on chronology in Alice Munro stories, which I suspected no one, not even my committee, had understood.

On the day of the interview, I arrived fifteen minutes early, freshly showered and lightly caffeinated. I assured the interviewer—a severe man I never encountered again—that I coped well with stress, that I didn't take my work home with me, that I sought help whenever I felt overwhelmed, that after watching horror films I slept deeply with soothing dreams of beaches and children frolicking in the surf. This person I'd concocted sounded like a sociopath. I got the job.

A calico cat with singed whiskers snarling at a man holding a candle to her face. A circumcised dick, an uncircumcised dick. A teenage boy daring another teenage boy to lick a horse's scrotum. Two women in vintage wedding veils kissing each other. Three men blustering for the return of slavery. A naked, blindfolded woman yelping in a cage.

I deleted and deleted, letting the wedding picture, a welcome flicker of happiness, stay. It didn't seem possible—I thought I'd reached a plateau of numbness—but the work was getting worse, the breaks a breathless sprint and the clicking hours a relentless slog. I'd been there for two and a half months. When I first started, I would plead with my supervisor to call the police, the government, anyone who could help these people, but she simply waggled her bob at me, bemused and condescending, and parroted the line about the company's privacy policy, referring to page thirteen of my employee manual.

Sometimes I recognized people: neighbours, former math teachers, cousins, friends—I once saw my father de-quilling a porcupine—but after a minute or so their noses would shift, their eyes would switch colour and they would become strangers.

"Ever seen anyone you know?" I asked a colleague, Martha, when we were drying our hands slowly in the bathroom. I would have asked Zoe, but she'd been ignoring me. Every time I tried to approach her, she would slither off on yet another break. Maybe she was ashamed of herself.

"My first month here I saw my husband fucking a poodle, my

daughter chugging bleach and myself jumping off the Golden Gate bridge," Martha said, giggling breathily.

I scowled at my reflection in the mirror. Where did those zits come from? Was one of my eyebrows more arched than the other?

"You get used to it," she continued, in a quieter more serious tone. "I've never actually seen anyone I know—I don't think. I go through everything so fast now, it's a blur." She threw her paper towel in the trash. "Just pretend it's a *Game of Thrones* episode. That's what I do."

After Martha left, I stood in the bathroom for a moment longer examining my face in the mirror, the constellation of freckles on the bridge of my nose drifting upward, my lower lip shrivelling.

I couldn't understand why Zoe had done this to me or why she refused to acknowledge my existence. Was it punishment for some thoughtless thing I'd said or done? Was it from back in high school? Did I give off a vibe of such profound detachment and mental toughness that she thought I wouldn't be affected by this? It was difficult to accept that she experienced the work any differently than I did. Anyone would be traumatized. If we commiserated, maybe the days would seem easier.

I wrote long email drafts, casting her as an executioner, a tyrant, a devil, begging her to be honest with me. Had I annoyed her or let her down? I came to work on time and I did my job so why was she treating me this way? My confused anger merged with some of the images on my screen. Bad thoughts involving pitchforks and blowtorches. The only way out of this oppressive feeling, the only way to achieve closure, I told myself, was to confront her.

I texted. I called. I got to work early and stayed late, lurking, hoping to corner her. And one morning, four months in, I got my chance when I spied her in the parking lot. I hustled to the front door and locking both hands to the frame, barred her entrance. She sighed, her frail body seeming to deflate.

"Fine," she said.

I almost hugged her, she looked so fragile. Seeing her standing there, I doubted my intentions, worried I was unfairly projecting all my rage and disappointment onto her, someone who was, after all, just a human woman, who was probably hurting, too. I blinked, trying to re-invoke a furious righteousness.

"Why?" I said in a tiny voice. "Why me?"

"Look," she said. "You can't tell anyone. Management only trusts a few of us. They think it would be bad for morale."

"What are you talking about?" I suspected she was going to hand me some pills, anti-anxiety meds or a micro-dose of MDMA. I welcomed the idea.

"The breaks," she said. "I can get you more breaks."

I removed my hands from the door frame.

"You just have to refer someone," she continued. "Anyone."

I closed my eyes and breathed hard.

"I use social media to recruit," she continued. "Whenever someone whines about their current job or mentions a recent firing, I send them a message, meet them for coffee and casually bring up the job, coach them on their interview, and if they're hired, I get another thirty-minute break."

Thirty minutes? That's all I was worth? And to think I'd met with her out of benevolence, believing she was as lonely as me.

"Most of them quit within the first two months, but apparently that's actually way, way better than the old turnover rate, back when the app still relied on job sites. And even if your person quits you still get the break. None of my other recruits has lasted as long as you."

I felt a sick and unwelcome surge of pride about my superior stamina. "I would never do that to someone," I said.

She rolled her eyes. "Sure, fine, whatever. I need to survive. I need to feed my kid. And there are worse jobs out there. We get paid well and we're doing a valuable service. Let's not get hysterical. This isn't grad school. We're all adults. Nice jacket by the way."

I looked down at my new leather jacket, the most expensive item of clothing I owned: buttery soft, the caramel colour so rich it almost glowed. Disgusted, I moved aside and let her enter the building.

I declined the few party invitations I got, then stopped receiving any. Small mercy I didn't have a spouse—my libido, never particularly robust, had withered entirely after the things I'd seen. I sometimes wondered if that's why Zoe and her husband had split up, but I couldn't speak to her, not yet. I didn't want access to intimacies that would nuance her and make it harder to maintain my anger. Still, if I could have, I would have asked if she thought the job had affected her relationship to her child, made her more vigilant or afraid as a parent. My future, weakly imagined and fading at an accelerating rate, no longer included kids. I wouldn't have been able to leave them with a babysitter, or with anyone, to ever let them out of my sight, not after my anxieties had been stoked by all the cruelty that skulked, undetected and unpunished, through the world.

I should have left the job, of course. And many evenings, half-thawed on Merlot, my computer warm on my lap, I searched through job advertisements, law school admission procedures and college program descriptions. I envisioned a life suffused with a sense of purpose and meaning and resolved to start anew, only to wake the next morning on the couch, hungover and overwhelmed by the immense effort such a change would require, those alternate selves dissolving in the sunlight.

I reassured myself that the job had important benefits. The pay was good, three times better than the contract teaching job I had before, good enough for me to buy a new car and to move into a bigger and less roach-infested place, and I liked being able to tell people, particularly my parents and former classmates, that I worked in tech now. I used the word *career*. It made my life sound fuller, plusher, as though I was riding an inevitable trajectory toward lasting affluence.

A man carving a name into a child's bare arm. A woman giving blow jobs to two men in army fatigues. A fat dick.

I closed my eyes for a moment, for several cleansing and replenishing minutes, then felt a familiar jab in my back. "Another hour before break time," my supervisor said. "Don't make me write a warning."

A skinny dick. Men screaming slurs at a woman wearing a headscarf.

At times like these, I could almost understand why Zoe had done what she'd done; not that I condoned it, but as the months went by it became easier to imagine doing it myself.

After work I went home and took a long, hot shower, scouring my crevices with apricot body wash. *A boy sticking a severed finger up his nose.* I poured myself a glass of Merlot, the good stuff from Napa Valley, told myself I would only drink one tonight. *A woman convulsing on the sidewalk, overdosing, while bystanders stand and watch.*

I tried to avoid screens during my off time but I still checked my email at least once a day. *Teeth being yanked out with pliers.* My former classmate Marian, a modernist who specialized in Woolf, had emailed me. The subject line read "A Teensy Request" and she wrote in a self-deprecatory style, jokiness and exclamation marks imperfectly masking an underlying desperation, to ask whether I had any leads on a job. She detailed the twenty campus interviews she'd gone to without success and said she'd heard I worked at the app now. That I was thriving.

I closed the laptop.

I was gratified to hear people were speaking about my life positively—using the word *thriving* in particular thrilled me— but I knew I had to tell her the truth, to warn her not to make the same mistake I did. Part of me wondered if this situation was different than my situation with Zoe. After all, Marian had approached *me*. It wasn't like I actively recruited her. *A Pomeranian lapping up a puddle of bloody vomit.* It would be passive, just letting something already in motion stay in motion. And from what I recalled, Marian was a resilient person, the first in our cohort to graduate, and I was pretty sure she'd told me she ran marathons and meditated. In many ways she would be the ideal candidate for the job.

Not that I would let her take it.

Still, I knew what it was like to be unemployed for a long time, how that uncertainty could be a kind of torture, particularly when you were simultaneously mourning the death of the life you'd always pictured for yourself. And the job really did have its perks. In a way, we were doing a noble service for the world—grunt work, dirty work, necessary, important and vital work.

I would write back and ask Marian to meet me for coffee so I could explain the challenges of the job. I would be as honest as possible; anything to help her make an informed choice about her future.

I tipped more Merlot into my glass and swirled it. With each sip, my mind felt cleaner.

THE UNOFFICIAL CALCULATION MUSEUM

+

George was worried about the calculators. They preferred a cool temperature, and the air conditioner—even after a few sound spanks—only managed a wheeze. Not yet nine a.m., it was already ninety degrees Fahrenheit outside. George called his sister Laurel and asked her to haul the rusty fan out of the garage. She didn't answer. Typical. Probably giving her right arm a workout at the slots. He considered driving home himself but hated the idea of opening late, especially since his collection of abacuses, slide rules and calculators had grown more popular after a young man dressed like George's grandfather—bow tie, tweed blazer, circular spectacles, corncob pipe—had posted pictures of George and his museum for a web page about unusual things to see in the area.

—

Two hours and three failed phone calls to his sister later, George was showing off one of his gems to a young couple. Sweat gathered under his armpits and collar, so he allowed himself to loosen his blue necktie.

"Check out the wizard!" the girl said. "He looks high!"

The calculator's casing was predominantly orange with purple keys. The screen was surrounded by a purple cloud below which there was a Santa Claus–like wizard with his eyes closed. He was pointing up, lightning zigzagging from his fingers.

"It's called a Wiz-A-Tron," George said, remembering both times he'd stolen it.

The first: he pocketed it off the line at the factory and spent the rest of the shift imagining his sister's reaction—her dimples big as hubcaps, a shriek of joy so loud it would set their mother's budgie squawking.

The second: he swiped it from one of his sister's cardboard boxes a few days after she'd moved in just to see if she'd notice, which she didn't. She'd never truly appreciated it, anyway.

Not all the calculators were acquired this way, but George's favourites were. Nevertheless, he didn't consider himself a thief nor, he believed, did others see him this way. Stealing, in his experience, was simply the best method to cope with life's disappointments.

"This place is surreal." The boy spun around and George, confused by the remark, tried to imagine what the room would look like from his perspective. He could see nothing surreal about it. It measured roughly thirty square feet, and George prided himself on its maintenance. The walls were honeysuckle white and the floors were waxed grey linoleum. Each calculating tool had been lovingly hung with an accompanying description—model, make and year, sometimes with a fun fact or two—typed on a pink index card. George's small desk stood opposite the door. Along the right wall were two boxy windows, one of which was mostly blocked by the useless air conditioner. They let in slashes of brightness, but overheads were still necessary to provide adequate reading light.

"So this Wiz was for kids?" the girl asked. George tried not to stare too hard at the tangerine glare of her lipstick. He didn't understand her outfit: a loose, grubby, ruffled pink dress, men's loafers and lime green socks.

"Yes," George said. "It's similar to the Little Professor but that one has a picture of a man with glasses under the screen. Both have the basic arithmetic functions. Add, subtract, multiply, divide."

"Doesn't this thing work?" The boy pointed at the air conditioner.

"Not at the moment." At what temperature would the calculators' internal functions be disrupted? The factory had been kept so frigid that George used to wear woollen socks and two or three extra undershirts beneath his uniform.

"Is it possible to open a window?" the boy said.

Wind smacked against the glass. "I'd rather not."

"Andy, don't you think we should do a documentary about this guy? Listen to this..." She looked down at an index card. Her voice became slanted and loud, on the edge of laughter. "*Wiz-A-Tron helped my sister appreciate the joy of long division and was instrumental in enabling her to achieve a C-plus in grade four arithmetic.* Fabulous, right? So earnest."

"It's literally ten trillion degrees in here, Sharon. How are you not dying?" The boy's thumbs twitched over a tiny screen. "Damn. No reception."

"Some like it hot."

Do they think I can't hear them? George wondered. *And what was so funny about his sister getting a C-plus?* He was starting to tire of this parade of young people, their assumptions, their seeming disinterest in calculators, their tattoos and stretched ear lobes. Why were they even here?

"Wait," Sharon said as she moved toward the TI-108 and read its explanation. "*This lovely piece is unusual for its bright blue casing, a colour I'd only ever seen before in my sister's eyes.*"

"Kinky," Andy said, then turned to George. "Why do you only write stuff about your sister, dude?"

George was about to say something when there was a loud jangle and the door swung open. Clouds of rust-coloured sand ballooned through the shop. George rushed into the chaos and flung his arms open as though in a hug. *Not my babies!* he thought as he hopped up and down, praying his body could catch all the particles.

From within the haze a snout appeared, then two satiny ears; finally, a mane of gold and pink sequins: a horse's head emblazoned on his sister's good luck sweater. She held a Big Gulp cup in her shaking left hand. Quarters spilled, plinking across the floor.

"The world is going to hell in a handbasket," she said as sand drifted, coating George's bald head, the boy's thick glasses and the girl's freckled shoulders.

George trembled with the thought of turning around and seeing the damage. Why would she open the door if she so much as suspected it might send sand swirling through his dream? Orange tears slid around his wrinkles. His sister could be such a thoughtless bitch.

X

George's blood felt thin and hot inside his body. He should have put his collection behind glass but he wanted people to feel close to the calculators. They weren't scary at all, not even the scientific and graphing ones. Not if you treated them properly and took the time to read the manuals. Got to know them.

He remembered sneaking up on eight-year-old Laurel as she sat cross-legged in the living room, holding the Wiz-A-Tron upright in one hand and a naked Barbie in the other.

"You're so smart," she'd said, jostling the Barbie up and down. "I love smart men. Let's kiss." She mashed the calculator and the Barbie together.

"I don't think that's how you use a calculator," he'd said.

Unembarrassed by his sudden appearance, she continued directing her eccentrically cast love scene. "Yes, but it's *why* you use one."

It saddened and angered George to think of his sister when she was still young and full of potential, a cheeky girl who starred in school plays and wrote an advice column for the paper under the pseudonym "Loretta Lovely." All that changed when she strutted into her first casino at eighteen on the arm of their married neighbour. She never did find a smart man of her own, settling instead for machines. Dumb ones, at that. Rather than answers or love, they provided whirls of apples, oranges, bananas and cherries.

To sate her addiction she'd spent all her inheritance and maxed out ten credit cards. She was always demanding money, even though he'd already let her move in with him; and besides, he was surviving on a pension and had the museum to keep up. It was disgraceful. But there was no solution as far as he could see. Therapy, self-help seminars, teary interventions: none of it worked. At least his calculators responded to his love and were their best selves around him, as long as he took the time to ask them some questions every so often.

÷

George began his inspection. The damage was extensive but not total. He blew on the casing of a T1-30 and could almost feel its weight in his pocket. He'd filched it the same day Laurel had graduated high school. Same night, that is. He'd begged for a night shift so that he could make it to the ceremony.

"Georgie Porgie," Laurel said. "Aren't you going to ask me why the world's going to hell in a handbasket?"

"Are you the famous sister?" Andy said.

Laurel grinned, seemingly unfazed by the question. "The famousest. You want my autograph, sugar lips?"

"I adore your equine shirt," Sharon said loudly.

"Thanks, sweetie," Laurel said. "It's my jackpot shirt."

George tried to ignore the others and concentrate on making the rounds. Nothing could save the HP-38E, but it wasn't one of his favourites. "At least dust can't mess up the slide rules and abacuses too badly," he said out loud, without meaning to.

"Too true, brother," Laurel said. "Darn, I'm sweating like a hog."

"Sharon, let's go," Andy said, moving toward George and the door. "This scene is starting to sketch me out."

"Where did you get your shirt?" Sharon said. "That horse is just so perfect. It would be fierce on my style blog. I wish I had my camera. Would you model for me?"

"On one condition," Laurel said.

"Condition?"

"Sweet cheeks has to be there, too."

"Who?"

"Him."

At this both Andy and George turned to see Laurel pointing in their direction. She winked her spidery eyelashes and blew a kiss, wiping the residual lipstick, a frosty pink, on the back pocket of her jeans. George felt his cheeks heat up. He was embarrassed, he told himself, because of his sister's vulgarity.

"Leave me out of this," Andy said. "I'm going."

"You can't go out there," Laurel said. "There's a tornado."

George dropped the calculator he was holding, a TI-56, and it clacked on the floor. "What's wrong with you? Why didn't you say so?"

"I did. World. Going to Hell. Handbasket."

"Where is it headed? Is it just a warning? Should we be going elsewhere? You're unbelievable."

"Well, excuse me for living. Al at the casino told me. That's why I came here: to save *you*."

The boy had his cell phone in his hand. He jabbed at the glowing screen. "Still no reception. Do you have a computer? We could check the news."

"No," George said.

"Isn't this a calculation museum?"

"We have to open the windows," Sharon said. "That's what you do for a tornado, right?"

"Honey pie, do you recall my entrance?" Laurel shook her cup. "We'll be getting big gulps of grit if we do that."

"Shouldn't we all be getting under the desk or going to a shelter, like in a school drill?"

"No shelter here," Laurel said. "And if you think a desk's going to save you, you're even more naïve than you look."

"We have to do something," the boy said. "I can't stay here."

"I'm kind of scared," the girl said.

Everyone stood in silence, sweating in the direction of the door. After a while George rummaged behind his desk and found a box and two rolls of toilet paper. He began removing the calculators from the wall, wrapping them in the toilet paper and then depositing them in the box. He would deal with the dust later. For the moment he had to busy his hands. Sharon and Andy conferred shrilly in a corner and Laurel headed for the back. The office chair let out an accommodating groan as she plopped herself on it and began counting out her winnings on the desk.

The wind bansheed outside and granules scraped the glass. It was soothing, putting away the calculators. It was as if he were on the line. *Routine can be deeply therapeutic,* he mused. *Maybe that's why Laurel likes her damn slots so much.*

"Can we re-enact this for the documentary?" Sharon said loudly. "I don't really go for reenactments, but this is wild."

"Sharon, you are too obsessed with your camera," Andy said. "It's like you're a witch and the camera's your familiar."

"I'm just making conversation so I don't have to think about how nature is trying to fling us to Oz right now. And at least I don't have a cell phone as a Siamese twin."

Were he and Laurel guilty of this couple's terrible pettiness? George asked himself. *Is a camera to a cell phone as a slot machine is to a calculator?*

Sharon sulked while Andy, perhaps bored with her, walked over to Laurel. "So are you one of the owners of this place?"

"Do I look like a cuckoo calculator nut to you?" The table was now covered in little piles of quarters, like silver buttons against the dark brown.

"Uh." He left his mouth open.

"Don't answer, handsome." Laurel pinched the boy's cheek, fuchsia talons digging into freckled flesh. "Just keeping looking pretty and we'll get through this mess together. Damn, I'm sweating like a rooster in a henhouse." Using a folded-up museum pamphlet, she fanned extravagantly beneath her armpits, causing the horse on her shirt to nod.

Andy rubbed his violated skin and took a step away just as George felt a tap on his back.

"What's an imaginary budget?" Sharon asked. She twirled her blonde hair around her finger, and when she removed it, the hair remained in a frizzy helix.

"I'm sorry about my sister," George stammered. "She can be too... too overly intimate with people. She shouldn't..."

"Who cares?" She rolled her eyes. "Andy can be too overly obnoxious with people. I want to hear more about this imaginary budget business." She pointed at a TI-99 that George had stolen the day Laurel got her braces off. "See, this card thingee says, *Mother would use this calculator to create imaginary budgets in order to teach my sister about finances.*"

"Ha!" Laurel snorted. "Imaginary schma-maginary."

Something large slapped the glass, momentarily obscuring the light. The girl yelped.

"It's essentially a dream budget," George said, not knowing how to reassure her. "You know, if she ever got rich, the things she would buy."

"Like?"

"Jewellery, perfume, things she heard about on the radio or

read about in magazines. Women's stuff."

"What a crock of shit," Laurel said.

"Excuse me," George said. "But could you please stop terrorizing my patrons?"

"Mother wasn't making imaginary budgets."

"You'll have to forgive my sister. She's not well."

Sharon shuffled toward Andy as Laurel continued to speak. "She was adding up the damage of another spending spree, soothing herself that her debt wasn't that bad and she deserved it and she'd worked for years and any day now Dad would get back and her debt would disappear and they'd waltz off into the sunset."

"Why do you have to be so nasty? She was a good woman. She had her problems."

"Understatement of the millennium."

George wished he were the kind of person who could walk over to the desk and push the quarters to the floor in a glittering waterfall. But he just wasn't that kind of guy, so instead he mumbled, "You're just like her."

"Duh."

Taken by surprise, George took several steps toward Laurel, and answered loudly, "Doesn't that bother you?"

"What bothers me is that you let me get away with it."

George rounded the desk. "It's not my job to fix your life. I'm not your father."

"Ever heard of deodorant?" She fanned her nostrils. "You're not my boyfriend either, you know. I never asked you for any of this." Opening both arms wide, she raised her chin and glanced brusquely around the room.

He faltered back, nearly tripping. The dimensions of the museum seemed to shift, becoming larger then smaller. *What was she talking about? What was he to her? Roommate. Bank. She was ungrateful, that's all. She didn't love him enough. Or: did he love her too much?*

When his eyes began to refocus, he noticed Sharon and Andy huddled in the centre of the room. A shiny purple rectangle lay on the floor between them, as though it were a shared organ with twin white cords leading to twin white earphones that were plugged into twin brains. George envied them. Lovers, that's what they were, protecting each other from nature's malice.

The air conditioner burbled. A thin tickertape of smoke floated between the grills. George took a deep breath and walked forward to investigate, glad to have something concrete to do. He felt a tug on his arm as Laurel yanked him backwards.

He fell to the floor. "Laurel, you can't keep—"

Orange and yellow sparks. A black-purple smear. The acrid tang of burnt plastic. All the heat of the day condensed into one moment as the air conditioner exploded.

=

The museum, untouched by the tornado, lost most of one wall in the air conditioner blast, but that was nothing compared to the natural disaster damage to the town. The casino had been reduced to a heap of still-blinking lights and overturned card tables; red and blue chips had soared as far as a mile away. Half of George's house was gone. Couches, smashed computers, books and broken glass clogged the streets. Young men and women stalked through the debris pointing their enormous lenses at eyeless teddy bears and dead goldfish. Power cords hung like snakes from branches.

Although George had not managed to save his eyelashes— they'd burned off in the blast—he'd managed to save the majority of his calculators and had hopes to start a new museum soon. His sister claimed to want to help. Neither of them ever mentioned the fight again; they never liked to relive such unpleasantness. She felt itchy these days, she told him. No slots to keep the hands occupied. Not even a working computer to gamble online. He said he understood.

He'd been lucky, he told everyone. Lucky, yes, but not entirely. He'd lost some of his most beloved calculators and worst of all, he'd never been able to find the Wiz-A-Tron. It wasn't in the box, and it wasn't in the charred mess left at the museum.

"What do you think happened to it?" he asked Laurel one morning as they drove slowly through the wreckage, scouting bigger locations for the new museum.

"Maybe it was stolen."

"By who?"

"That couple obviously. That chick had a shifty look about her. She probably slipped it into her pocket."

"She didn't seem the stealing type." George said.

"Are you kidding me? And that boyfriend of hers—what a clown."

"I thought he was just your type," George teased.

Laurel smacked him playfully. "I've got to admit that girl had taste. She loved my jackpot shirt, didn't she? Wanted me to be in a magazine! It must've been her. Not that I'm blame-gaming. Who could resist? It's pretty much the world's best calculator."

George glanced over at his little sister, and although he would later doubt himself, would wonder if he was projecting or thinking wishfully, at that moment he swore he saw a plastic orange angle poking out of his sister's purse. A wizard's eyes, serenely shut.

UNCLE HARRIS

Gavin only forgot one of his lines—the one about how people in Iceland consider him a delicacy—but a smiling teacher whisper-yelled it to him from the wings. Bill stole the show as the flamingo standing on one leg for twenty minutes and sneaking triumphant glances at his friend Henry, the vulture, whose curved foam beak kept falling off. I hooted and stomped as they bowed and bowed and bowed. Afterward we ate brownies and lemon squares in the gym, and I informed inquisitive parents and teachers that our mom had gone to the washroom and would be out any minute now.

I never used to lie about her. Back when it was all starting, I would say, "She's running," or, "She's circuit training." I was proud of her for losing all that weight after the divorce, for getting up every morning at five a.m. to put on her swishy nylon shorts with the deep slits up the sides. But after a while I could sense these weren't stellar explanations for why she hadn't shown up to parent-teacher conferences. Other moms, I noticed, managed to fit both Pilates and potlucks into their schedules.

When we got home, Mom was lying on the couch, a bag of frozen peas thawing on her pillow-propped ankle. I tried not to look at her toenails: ten black mood rings.

"Mom, Mom," Gavin said. "I can carry up to ten fish in my beak."

"I eat mostly algae and I can balance on one leg for an hour," said Bill, demonstrating the flamingo stance.

"That's great." Mom winced.

I told myself not to express sympathy, that it was all her own fault, but she just looked so frail and pathetic that I relented and asked if she needed anything.

"No," she said. "You go relax, honey."

On my way out of the room, she said, "Could you give your brothers their baths tonight? I'm just not up to it."

Without turning around, I said, "Yes."

Locking the door behind me, I sat on my galaxy-printed duvet and opened my laptop. Half an hour until my brothers' scheduled bathtub warfare. Enough time to scroll through some posts on TOIL AND TROUBLE FOR BEGINNERS. My friend Amy and I were learning everything we could before this coven meet up we'd heard about next month. We already had outfits planned: crushed black velvet skirts, rings on every finger, silver Doc Martens. Amy had even been watching YouTube makeup tutorials on perfecting cat eye swoops of liquid eyeliner to make us look older, at least sixteen.

I was reading about phases of the moon—*Disseminating moon, associated with divorce, emotional turmoil*—when I heard the doorbell ringing, a spacy *bo-bo-bleep*. Probably a Jehovah's witness or a Girl Guide or something—*and also commonly known to exacerbate addictions*.

"Can you get that, Chrissie?" Mom yelled.

I ignored her, confident that whoever it was would get the message and leave. But the doorbell kept ringing, derailing my concentration and forcing me to reread the same sentence. *Disseminating moon, associated with divorce, emotional turmoil…*

"Chrissie!"

"Can't Gavin or Bill do it?" I yelled down.

"Don't be silly."

"Silly, silly," Bill wriggled his way into my room. "Flamingos can't answer doors."

"People in Iceland consider me a delicacy," Gavin said, launching himself onto my bed. "Yummy. Puffin pudding. Puffin fingers. Puffin pot pie."

"Fine." I shut the laptop, shooed the boys into the hallway and stomped down the stairs. The ringing seemed to be getting louder, more insistent. I peered through the peephole. Standing there with a scowl on his face and a suitcase by his feet was Uncle Harris, my dad's brother, a man I hadn't seen since I was six years old.

Mom launched into hostess mode, hobbling around to procure tea and crackers. Uncle Harris declined to eat, drink or explain his presence.

"It's been a long day." He blinked to keep his eyes from closing.

"Did he tell you that she's stinking rich?" Mom asked, pulling the couch into a bed. "Oil money, diamond money. Something bloody."

"Chrissie," he said, forcing the words out. "What grade are you in now?"

"Nine," I said.

"Nine," he said. "Trigonometry?"

"Not yet."

Uncle Harris just nodded, sinking deeper into his seat. He didn't even attempt to engage Gavin and Bill, which was strange. Normally adults praise or tease small children, if only to impress other adults with their charm and wit. My dad, for one, never met a kid he didn't subject to a knock-knock joke or a nose heist. The boys clung to my legs, probably frightened of Uncle Harris, who was a gaunter, paler and more serious version of our father.

I took Gavin and Bill upstairs for their bath. Having shed their bird selves, they splashed and wriggled in the soapy water, occasionally halting their battle to discuss Uncle Harris. Who was he? Was he married? Did he have kids? Why had they never met him? I couldn't answer. I remembered him visiting once with a thin, perfumed woman and how tense Dad had been for weeks leading up to it, yelling at me to put away my toys, scrubbing and dusting and polishing, filling the air with fumes that made me dizzy.

Gavin and Bill concocted their own backstories out of my silence. Uncle Harris was a gazillion-year-old vampire with a ghost for a wife and a gazillion vampire-ghost children, and he'd just gotten out of jail for robbing a candy store and a bank and a diamond store. Or he was a childless, rich businessman whose wife had just died and he had come to give us all his money, enough money to fill a bathtub, a pool, the whole ocean.

The smell of bacon lifted me from moon-drenched dreams. In the kitchen, Uncle Harris, his waist cinched by a frilly teal apron, was draping strands of spitting meat on paper towels and flipping pancakes. A stern, miserable expression was on his face. I tried not to laugh.

"Looks great," I said.

"Take a seat," he said. "It's almost ready."

My place at the table had been set: a knife and fork, a glass of orange juice, even a napkin.

"When I got back from the store," Uncle Harris said, his back to me. "Marlene's car was gone."

"Yoga," I said. "Pilates, maybe circuit training. I forget her schedule."

"I thought she was injured." He deposited a stack of pancakes in front of me, bacon heaped on them like a gummy smile. "Does she leave you alone often?"

"I'm almost fourteen."

Gavin and Bill whirled into the room. Uncle Harris tensed, preparing their plates.

He put their breakfast down in front of them. "Did you sleep well, gentlemen?"

"I was a space spider from Jupiter," Gavin said.

"Me too!" Bill added.

Uncle Harris nodded gravely as though this were a revelation of some importance. He took a place at the head of the table. "Apologies," he said, pointing at the syrup. "It's fake."

"Do you have a wife?" Gavin asked.

"Yes," Uncle Harris said, flaring a napkin on his lap and picking up his knife and fork, his posture stiff and proper.

"Where is she?" Bill said.

"In a big house taking a nice, long rest."

"Why?"

"She's sad."

"Why?"

"Adult worries," Uncle Harris said, already exhausted by the interrogation.

To relieve Uncle Harris of what he clearly felt were his uncle duties, I asked Bill and Gavin to explain their dreams to me, and they rambled on and on between bites. Big, messy, eager bites. The pancakes were light and fluffy, the bacon crisp and the syrup, corn rotting on the stalk.

In the week after Uncle Harris took over care of the house I realized how bad things had gotten, how bad I'd let them get. The living room carpet transformed from beige to white. Peanut butter sandwich dinners were replaced with roasted chicken, grilled asparagus and brown rice. The bathtub drain, freed from its hair gag, gulped down water again. I was grateful, but also embarrassed. Did he think we were filthy? And what about me? Had I failed? I could see now that washing a few dishes and tying a few shoelaces weren't enough to be a real adult. But he couldn't deny I'd done a good job with the boys. He continued to treat Bill and Gavin with intimidated deference as though they were domesticated bears or foreign dignitaries.

With fewer household duties, I was able to devote myself more seriously to preparing with Amy. We watched *The Craft* and painted our fingernails black. We lit candles and sandalwood incense and intoned our spells. Nothing too serious yet, though, just spells to help us pass a French test or to guarantee a good hair day. After careful discussion, we'd agreed we shouldn't anger the spirits by messing with the important spells—the love spells—until we'd learned more.

"We're not just doing this as a fad," Amy said solemnly. "People don't realize that Wicca is a legitimate religion. It should be treated with respect."

"Right," I said. "Want to look at some more pictures of those crystal amulets on Pinterest?"

Without telling Amy, I'd started practising some of the more skilled spells. One night I took a wedding picture of my mother and father out of a photo album and drew a pentagram on it, then I rolled it up and put it in a mason jar along with crushed tulip petals and a splash of vanilla extract. I buried it in the back garden and waited for Dad to come home.

Two weeks after I cast the spell I went to collect Gavin and Bill after school as usual but was told that they'd already left with my father. I was so happy I nearly cried. Dad was back. He could talk sense to Mom, make her laugh so hard she forgot to be anxious. That woman in Florida was just a blip. *The spell had worked!*

As I walked home I wondered if Uncle Harris would be happy or sad about Dad's return. He'd been with us for almost three weeks, cleaning and cooking, reading his politician biographies in the evening and trying to summon the courage to question my mother.

"Has a physician advised you to exercise so much?" he'd ask.

"My naturopath tells me I'm on the path to my best self," she'd reply.

Uncle Harris would squint and clench his jaw at these non-answers but never pushed back. He was like some repressed minister from another century. Once when he was on the computer I looked over his shoulder and saw that he'd been googling jokes. The next day he stopped the boys in the hallway.

"Why was the tomato embarrassed?"

"He lost a ketchup fight," Bill said.

"He didn't have any friends," Gavin said. "He was a stinky weirdo."

"He saw the salad dressing," Uncle Harris said, chortling to himself.

The boys, to my surprise, laughed along with him, clutching their chests, tears in their eyes, trying—I assumed—to make Uncle Harris feel better for being so uncool.

When I got home I found Dad sitting in the living room, Gavin and Bill cross-legged at his feet. But when I got closer, I saw that it wasn't Dad at all. It was only Uncle Harris, a looser Uncle Harris with a goofy grin messing up his face. He was holding a thick book and reading from it in a strained, nasal tone then a halting, stuttered one. The boys cackled at his voices. He'd probably learned the whole routine from some YouTube video.

"Where's Dad?" I said.

Uncle Harris stopped. He seemed annoyed by the interruption, but also like he was struggling to suppress this annoyance.

"In Florida," Bill said.

"Very funny," I said. "The teacher told me he picked you up from school. Is he in the bedroom? The backyard?"

Uncle Harris shook his head. "Sorry to disappoint, but that was me."

"You?"

"I picked them up. When we were younger, people could barely tell your father and me apart."

"Keep reading," Gavin said.

I sighed and went to my room to blast music, anything to drown out the sound of Uncle Harris's performance, or whatever you wanted to call his pathetic attempt to win over his nephews.

It was bad enough that the boys betrayed me by pretending to like Uncle Harris's try-hard rendition of *The Hobbit*, giggling away like idiots, but Mom soon took to listening, too, sprawled on the couch after a gruelling workout, interjecting with questions, only to be shushed by one of the boys.

One night after dinner, I cornered her in the kitchen while she was grabbing a coconut water from the sparkling and ruthlessly organized fridge.

"What exactly is he doing here?"

"He's helping out," she said. "He has a sense of obligation and responsibility. Unlike his brother."

"But why does he care about us all of a sudden?"

"His wife is sick."

"So he should be with her."

"It's not that easy," she said. "You'll understand when you're older."

"Did you call him?"

She gulped her drink. "You should really try this stuff. It's great for your skin."

"He's not going to leave her for you," I said. "Just so you know."

"Don't be such a little bitch."

I was too stunned to respond and I wouldn't have had a chance to anyway because Uncle Harris appeared in the doorway.

"Marlene," he said in a scolding tone, angrier than I'd ever heard him.

Her neck and face exploded in red blotches and she bowed her head, a chastened child.

"Chrissie," he said.

"It's Christina," I replied. "And this is between me and my mother. You can go back to the living room and keep playing house."

"That's your territory. You and your mother and father. I live in the real world."

I told myself not to react, vowed to curse him, hex him, send all the demons of the world his way. He didn't care about us, not really. He wanted to feel superior to his brother, superior to us. He wanted to screw up our lives, turn us all against each other. As though sensing some danger, Gavin and Bill danced into the kitchen.

"Mom, why was the tomato scared?" Gavin said.

I turned and left the room. On my way up the stairs, I heard Bill deliver the punchline: "Because he saw the lettuce naked."

The next morning Uncle Harris apologized for what he'd said the day before. "You've done an excellent job," he said. "Considering… considering everything. I had no right to say that."

I pretended to accept his apology, but inside I fumed and raged. I scrolled through all the darkest corners of TOIL AND TROUBLE but nothing was dark enough. I searched elsewhere, every witch site I could find, bookmarking curses that would cause boils to erupt on his skin, sorrow to eat at his soul, spiders to consume his dick. The anger gave me a purpose, a dense centre to circle my thoughts around.

I pressed Gavin and Bill to tell me what the three of them talked about.

"Mount Doom!" Gavin said. He was wearing a shirt I didn't recognize, an orange polo with a tiny zebra stitched on the chest.

Had Uncle Harris started buying them clothes now, too? Wasn't it enough for him to make the laundry smell like a mountain spring and to clean the windows so thoroughly that birds crashed into them?

"And?"

"The ring!" Bill said, imitating the gravelly voice Uncle Harris sometimes used when he read.

"And? His wife? His house?"

"He has a big backyard," Gavin said.

"And a pool," Bill added. "He said one day he'd take us there."

I grabbed Bill's shoulder. "When?"

"He says it a lot," Bill said. "Maybe you can come, too!"

"Don't ever leave without telling me or Mom okay?"

"Die, dragon," Gavin said, poking his index finger into my stomach.

Falling to the floor in mock agony, I wondered if I was strong enough, witch enough, to curse him. I thought about the useless jar I'd buried in the backyard.

The morning before the coven meet-up, Gavin and Bill burst into my room. I hadn't joined them for breakfast. I didn't want to eat Uncle Harris's pancakes or omelettes or stacks of French toast with their pretentious dusting of nutmeg.

"Are you coming to school tonight?"

"Why?" I said. *Would the other people at the coven be older? Cooler? Would they offer me red wine or marijuana or magic mushrooms?*

"It's Games Night!" Bill said. "I'm going to beat Henry and Gavin and Uncle Harris at darts."

"I'm going to smash, bash, crush the piñata until it poops candy," said Gavin.

Games Night was an annual tradition at their school, one I remembered well from being a kid. Dad let me win at everything, and afterward my reward was to get a piggyback ride all the way home.

"Sorry, guys." I ruffled their hair. "I have other plans." I was going to find the most powerful witch and ask her to help me banish Uncle Harris from the house.

"Uncle Harris says whoever wins the most games gets to choose a prize."

"I'm getting a waterslide," Gavin said.

"Cool," I said. "Now be gone! You're going to be late."

After school I went straight to Amy's, but I was distracted. We changed into our outfits. The velvet itched my skin and the boots suddenly seemed clunky and oversized, like clown shoes. Sandalwood incense swarmed my throat. Amy was talking about binding spells and the many therapeutic uses of quartz. I pictured the mason jar vibrating in its backyard grave, rotten tulip petals whirring, my newlywed parents grabbing and shaking the penta-gram lines, trying to free themselves. I could barely breathe. *What exactly was Gavin planning to do with a waterslide?* Amy applied eyeliner to herself and then tried to get me to hold still while she applied some on me. *Use it at Uncle Harris's pool?* With one eye shakily lined, I excused myself, rushing out of Amy's house while she yelled after me.

I pushed my way through the parents and kids and scanned the gym for Uncle Harris's lanky frame, his tweed coat. I poked my head under a parachute. I checked underneath the snacks table. I was just about to bust into the boys' washroom when I saw Mom dressed in actual non-Spandex clothes for once. She wore a blazer and jeans, even cute yellow flats; her hair was blow-dried and her lips were lipsticked.

Bill and Gavin ran over and hugged me.

"What happened to your eye?" Mom said. "And what are you wearing?"

"Where's Uncle Harris?"

"It was time for him to go," she said.

"Did you kick him out?"

"Don't be so dramatic. He had to go. He wanted me to tell you goodbye."

"But," I said. "Why would he just leave?"

"His wife was being discharged," she said.

"But—"

"Leave it."

I could sense she wasn't telling me everything but I didn't press her further, too frazzled to care about the details and enjoying Mom's mom-like tone, authoritative for once. It seemed strange that he hadn't said goodbye to me. Could he feel how angry I was? Was I the reason he left?

Mom and Bill went to wait in line for some game and I challenged Gavin to a beanbag toss. A low ringing filled my ears, getting louder and more insistent. Gavin grabbed the hem of my skirt and blew his nose on it, leaving a thick mucus slug clinging to the velvet hairs. On the other side of the room, Bill reached for Mom's hand, which kept slipping in and out of his as she raised herself onto the tips of her toes and lowered herself again, mouthing the rep count under her breath.

THE EMILIES

Every morning before work Emily straightens her hair and curls her eyelashes. She alternates between Sparkling Lilac Mystic and Sea Breeze Clean Burst antiperspirant because she can't decide whether floral or fresh scents best express her authentic self. Around her neck she wears a tiny gold heart on a thin gold chain. She irons her clothes every Friday night, even the jeans she only wears on weekends. Everything in order. People often ask her to speak up.

Emily has two friends. Both are ceremonial holdovers from elementary school. Friendships as dutiful and potentially pointless as washing dishes before putting them in the dishwasher. Emily wants more. She wants a friendship that's a perpetual scooping of chocolate chip cookie dough ice cream. One long pillow fight. A continuous revelation of secret crushes. The kind of friendship with inside jokes, with whole days spent texting smiley faces to one another. But there doesn't seem to be room in her friends' lives for this kind of friendship. Both her friends have boyfriends. When Emily calls them, she can sense their hesitation. They make excuses, drop her for incoming calls. It's obvious she's become a burden. And it's not as if they're exactly her first choice for bosom buddies, but what other option does she have?

Emily has more namesakes than friends. Her mother named her after three Emilies, specifically: Brontë, Dickinson and Davison. Two of them, literary recluses. The other, trampled to death by a king's horse. All beloved by feminists and all single, like Emily. Probably virgins like her, too. Whenever Emily is stuck in some expanding moment of socially induced panic—her breath coming on faster, the inner voice goading *speak up, you're sweating, touch him, hug her, do something for fuck's sake*—she tells herself not to worry; it's just a case of the Emilies. The naming of this awkwardness consoles her, makes it pathological, flings the blame out centrifugally, away from the self of herself. A self best expressed with deliberation over what she can control: clothes that flatter her mildly pear-shaped body, the perfect shade of blush, periods every twenty-eight days on the dot. Despite her virginity, despite the fact that she's only been out on one date and never even kissed the guy, Emily has been on birth control since the eleventh grade. She couldn't bear the uncertainty of irregular menstruation. The body is untrustworthy, full of potential mutinies.

Emily works at Phil's Consulting, a small firm in downtown Ottawa that specializes in strategic planning for non-profit organizations. The other four employees are Tony, Roger, Mary and Lydia. Phil of Phil's Consulting is short not for Philip, but for Philanthropic, an abbreviation that Roger says makes the company seem "more approachable" and Tony claims makes it sound "snazzier."

Lydia, the employee closest in age to Emily, has been working there for two years, a year and a half longer than Emily. Lydia's business cards are gilt-edged and read, *Assistant Project Improvement Officer*. Emily's are plain white and read, *Assistant Project Enhancement Officer*. Emily has been promised she will get gilt-edged cards after she's been there for a year.

When Emily first started her job, she enjoyed the work. All she did was copy-edit reports before they were sent out to the clients, yet she derived satisfaction from her association, however tangential, with the important philanthropic work being done. Lately, though, the routine of it, the tedium and isolation of spending so many hours editing and re-editing a single sentence, has strained her. Even more than the work itself, the office environment has stoked her Emilies.

On her first day, wishing to give the impression she was someone with a vital and fulfilling personal life, she'd brought a framed picture of her and her girlfriends from prom: their hair curled and, beneath their dresses, their stomachs sucked in. She'd placed it on her desk before noticing that Mary was the only other person with photos on display. She was about to hide it when Roger ambled over and picked it up.

"Looking pretty smart," he said. "College?"

"High school." Emily tried for nonchalance. "My best friends."

"You haven't changed a bit."

Roger put the frame down. Emily cringed at the coarse, curly hair on the backs of his fingers.

"Better pretend I work here," he said.

He winked and walked over to his corner of the office. Following this exchange, Emily worried that it would be too conspicuous now to remove the picture so she left it where it was.

Later that day, she attended a short introductory meeting with the rest of the employees. Emily took an empty seat beside Lydia. She found Lydia intimidating, though she couldn't have specified why. Definitely wasn't her looks. Her hair was part greasy, part frizzy. She did have a striking face: huge, protruding eyes and small, heart-shaped lips. She didn't wear makeup. At the meeting everyone was boisterous and friendly. They were all dressed casually, more casually than Emily had expected. Roger wore wrinkled khakis and a bulky light blue sweater. Tony wore black jeans and an open, plaid, button-down shirt with a black T-shirt underneath. Mary wore tapered charcoal trousers—polyester with a slight sheen—and a lime green, short-sleeved shirt, untucked.

But it was Lydia who struck Emily as the most egregious case. Lydia's knee-length jean skirt was hemmed unevenly with safety pins. Her faded, black cardigan was too small, buttons popping open across her breasts. Emily would never show up to work looking so unprofessional. Her smugness dissipated as banter buzzed and spun around her like a swarm of bees. She had trouble concentrating on individual voices.

The majority of the meeting was spent sharing anecdotes about the previous Assistant Project Enhancement Officer. Emily didn't remember all the details. Mostly she remembered the ironic look on Lydia's face, the easy flow of words from her mouth.

"Remember those fruit leathers she used to eat?" Lydia said. "She would lick those things like a cat."

"I'm just glad I won't have to smell her perfume anymore," Roger said. "Awful stuff. I'm allergic, you know."

"We know," Lydia said.

"She had the nicest penmanship," Mary said. "You can't teach penmanship like that."

"She had other assets," Tony said.

"Oh please." Lydia looked disgusted. "Can't you recognize a padded bra when you see one?"

Listening to Lydia talk, Emily was struck by a need to align herself with her. She'd never known someone so audacious and self-assured. Emily's desire for Lydia's recognition was overwhelming. It seemed to condense the room down to the two of them. Emily wished that she'd known this previous employee so she could gossip about her, too. Gossip viciously, like girls do. Like friends do, drawing a boundary between themselves and everyone else.

"Jealous?" Tony challenged Lydia.

Emily tried to cut in, her mouth open, poised, but couldn't find an opportunity.

"You got me," Lydia said sarcastically. "What more could any woman want out of life than a D cup and a dunce cap?"

"Children, children," Roger said. "Can we please *try* to stick to the agenda?"

By the end of the meeting, Emily noticed that she'd chipped off all her nail polish. She'd stacked the thin sheets of discarded varnish on top of each other. Looked like a hunk of mica.

Emily sat with her new colleagues at the round table in the small kitchen nook. She fumbled at the microwave, trying to figure out which setting to use to heat up her portion-controlled cayenne pepper and celery soup.

Tony sidled up to her. "Need a little help defrosting?" he said, draping his arm on her shoulder.

Emily winced. She prefers to be warned before anyone touches her. Taken aback, Tony removed his arm and muttered, "Sorry."

"Don't mind him," Lydia said dryly. "It's not called Philanderer's Consulting for nothing."

Mary smiled. Roger guffawed. Tony groaned.

"Oh," Emily said.

Routine insulated the relationships at the office. Agendas, reports. Emily continued to admire Lydia's confidence and to question her taste. Memos, clients, coffee. Fridays, the plate on Mary's desk began with baked goods and ended with crumbs. Photocopier jams. Roger told Emily that she'd "mastered the fine art of punctuation."

One day after Emily had been there five months, Mary called Lydia, "Emily." Realizing her mistake, she said, "Sorry, I always get you two mixed up."

Emily smiled and looked over at Lydia, who frowned.

Emily puzzled over that frown. What did it mean? The Emilies volunteered theories. *You're too awkward and shy. She thinks you're*

ditzy. A kinder Emily suggested, *Lydia doesn't know you yet...*
she doesn't like being compared to anybody. She thinks of herself as
unique, one of a kind. An iconoclast like us, a Brontë or a Dickinson
or a Davison.

That was exactly what made her so attractive.

Emily is eating her container of ten raw almonds when Lydia
whirls into the break room. She is wearing jeans, a white T-shirt
and a navy blazer with the sleeves pushed up to the elbows. She
doesn't look at Emily, concentrating instead on pouring herself a
cup of coffee.

"What you up to tomorrow afternoon?" Lydia asks.

Although she's alone, Emily is unsure whether she is being
addressed. "Me?"

"What?"

"I'm free." Emily can't believe this. She holds her hands still in
her lap, tries to keep her smile small.

"I assumed so. Can you come with me for this procedure thingee?" Coffee spills over the rim of the mug. Lydia stops pouring
but doesn't bother wiping the puddle.

"Sure. What—"

"A routine abortion. Tomorrow after work then?"

"It's a date," Emily says, immediately regretting her eagerness.

Lydia nods and exits, leaving the full coffee on the counter,
steam rising.

That night Emily, flattered by the afternoon's conversation, tries to
imagine how Lydia must be feeling. How Lydia must despise the
tampon ads on television. The white-clad women twirling around,
cooing about absorbency and freshness, spilling blue liquid everywhere. And of course, she wonders about the guy, if he's ever shown
his face around the office and if he knows about the pregnancy or
not. But mostly she wonders about Lydia. Is she lonely, too?

"At least there aren't any protesters today," Emily says as she and Lydia walk up the front stairs of the Morgentaler Clinic.

A pair of teenage girls are leaving. "So you won't tell anyone?" Lydia whispers. One of the girls leans heavily on the other.

"Of course not," Emily says. She's promised three times in the past forty-five minutes.

"Who would you tell, anyway?" Lydia smiles.

Emily brushes the question off as another example of Lydia's biting humour. "Right."

Emily had imagined that this experience would be intimate and vulnerable, like an after-school special, that it would cement a bond between them. But now that she's here, part of her wants to flee. All those bodies in there, leaking their secrets. Spilling their guts. She pictures a bedpan brimming full of miniature organs, secreting, throbbing, uncoiling and uncoiling. She climbs the steps ahead of Lydia and opens the door.

Inside the air is solemn. As they walk down a hall, Lydia's flip-flops come down in smacks, Emily's heels in clicks. They walk to the front desk. On the counter Lydia holds her left hand over her right to stop it from trembling. Emily notes Lydia's bitten cuticles. When the nurse asks for Lydia's name, she looks lost, so Emily answers for her.

"Please take a seat," the nurse says.

Another pair of girls sits in a corner. Their voices are low, sloshing against each other in a gentle rhythm. Lydia takes a seat and hunches behind a *Times*. As there's no available chair next to Lydia, Emily sits across from her. She reads a *Sass* from fall 2002. The words *sexy*, *secret* and *diet* are used among photos of elfin celebrities with prominent collarbones. After a few minutes, a wiry nurse with a stiff clipboard calls, "Lydia Mayes!" from across the room.

Lydia and Emily stand up and walk toward the nurse. Emily gets there first.

"Lydia?" the nurse says.

"No," Lydia says. "*I'm* Lydia."

"You'll have to stay here then," the nurse tells Emily.

"I'm coming, too," Emily says, emboldened by the dread in Lydia's eyes. "She needs me."

"I'm sorry," the nurse says. "That won't be possible."

"It's okay, Emily." Lydia doesn't look at her. "I'm fine."

"I'm right here," Emily says.

The nurse escorts Lydia to the back.

Sass recommends a hotel where you can shower in champagne and flounce around all day in bright dresses with low necklines. It says that Grey Goose martinis are fabulous and that purple crocodile, elbow-high gloves are both luxurious and demure. *Right now,* Emily thinks, *Lydia is probably putting her feet into stirrups. Soon the doctor will guide a tube into her uterus.*

When Lydia returns to the waiting area, Emily leaps from her seat, only to find that her arms won't open into a hug. *It's time to console her,* the Emilies declare, *to acknowledge Lydia's grief and introduce it to a sample of Emily's own.* Instead, she pictures Lydia entwined in ropes of blood, an umbilical cord crown on her head. Mimicking Lydia's briskness, Emily follows her into the corridor.

"Just wait a minute," Lydia says, ducking into an alcove. She leans against a wall, hanging her head. Lydia's cheeks are so blatantly and disastrously white that it occurs to Emily that she can help her by just acting like everything's normal. She offers her some blush.

"My whole universe got better when I learned to apply blush properly," Emily says. She thinks of the words as a kind of self-parody, compressing her personality down to something bite-sized, easily digestible. Expected. She retrieves a massive brush from her purse. "Ripe sunset, the perfect shade for you." She wants to give Lydia back the control of her body. To make her impenetrable again.

Lydia doesn't protest. With shimmering peach powder, Emily sculpts a cheekbone onto the left side of her face, careful not to touch her skin directly with her fingertips. Before she can start on the right, Lydia pushes Emily's arm away.

"At least let me make it symmetrical," Emily says. The thought of Lydia walking around only half-finished panics her. Everyone will notice something is wrong.

"I just want to get out of here."

With a movement as abrupt and necessary as a sneeze, Emily hugs Lydia. She feels the pain shivering through Lydia's body and she's prepared to share it. To let its unruliness pass from Lydia's body into her own. Lydia is hot and smells of soap. This isn't so bad, Emily thinks, this is what being a friend really is. Handing over control. Supporting them on their own terms. Emily hugs and hugs her. She moves her hand in circles on her back. Lydia's hands hang by her sides.

Emily is alone in the glow of her television, painting her finger-nails pink with white crescents at the tips. She looks back over the afternoon, returning each time to the hug. In the throes of it, she'd been free from the clutter and slap of the Emilies' judgment. She'd barely thought. It wasn't until Lydia was out of sight, the bus door wheezing shut, that Emily noticed the mucus on her shoulder. She wiped it off with a Kleenex.

The hosts of the show are in a woman's house, guffawing in front of her open closet. There are T-shirts with Disney characters on them. There are purple polyester pants, long sheer dresses with fur trim and paint-stained stonewashed tapered jeans. All in the same closet! Sequined tube tops, floral frocks and rainbow suspenders. On shelves to the side, fishnet tights and holey toe socks. The hosts want the woman to get rid of it all. The woman sags. She objects.

All seems lost until, suddenly, miraculously, the woman is throwing things out. She realizes nothing in the closet fits. There is fast, frantic camera work. Music blares. It's religious. She is converted. A close-up shows her clenching wads of fabric and cramming them into garbage bags. Black plastic distends and stretches clear. The music develops a steady electronic beat. The hosts smile with their inhumanly white teeth. The woman sways with unfocused frenzy. Everything is too big or too small. Everything is stained or see-through or clings to her love handles. She has seen the truth! She wants to change! Everything she owns pops open at the boobs or is slack in the crotch. Nothing is her! God, who is she? She is someone who could become someone else if she bought new clothes and got her hair cut in jagged layers and learned how to apply highlighter cream just below her eyebrows!

Emily doesn't get an opportunity to speak to Lydia all morning. Lydia appears to be swamped with work. She has a frazzled, do-not-disturb expression on her face. Emily is surprised—almost dismayed—to see Lydia wearing the same old outfit: black cardigan, corduroy skirt. How could anything stay the same? When Emily looks at the picture of her high school friends, she barely recognizes their faces. They have nothing to do with her. She lays the frame down flat on her desk.

In the afternoon, there is a goodbye party for Tony. He's leaving the office for a job at an office down the hall. As far as anyone can tell, his new job is more or less identical to his current one. It's no improvement or enhancement. Nevertheless, to celebrate his moving sideways in the world, they decide to eat grocery store sheet cake and drink sparkling grapefruit juice.

Lydia puts Bob Marley on so loud it's hard to think. *No woman, no cry.* Mary turns the music down so low it's a murmur, a suggestion of ocean waves. Tony and Roger swap statistics. Baseball or hockey. Roger produces a flask and pours something clear into Tony's cup, then waggles the flask at Lydia who rolls her eyes and extends her cup. This worries Emily. Lydia shouldn't be drinking in her condition, still fresh with grief.

Between mouthfuls of pastel icing, Mary tells Emily about her son's peanut allergy. Emily nods and asks appropriate questions about EpiPens and food labelling, thinking only of Lydia's presence, where she is in the room, how she's feeling. She breaks away from the conversation when she notices Lydia in the corner alone, cutting herself some cake.

"That looks great," Emily says, pointing at Lydia's slice decorated with lopsided baby blue rosettes.

Lydia sighs and turns to Emily. "Nice necklace," she says as though she is talking to a seven-year-old. "Is it new?"

"Sort of," Emily replies. It's a gold heart on a gold chain. Before Lydia can interrupt, Emily adds, "So do you want to maybe go see a movie this weekend? Or go shopping?"

"I can't," Lydia says. "I have a date."

Emily tries not to look disappointed.

"Honestly," Lydia says softly. "I do."

Although Emily understands that Lydia is lying, that—like Emily's other two friends—she is trying to brush her off, she can't help herself from pursuing the issue, however desperate she might seem. "What about next week?"

"We'll see," Lydia says.

She's still wounded and recovering, Emily tells herself. We went through something big together and that has to mean something.

"If you'll excuse me," Lydia says. "I need to take a piss."

Waiting a minute to make it less obvious, Emily follows Lydia to the washroom. Would they ever be the kind of friends who go together, who hand each other tampons or extra squares of toilet paper underneath the stall?

Lydia is at the sink washing her hands. "Hey," she says, without looking up.

Water rushes sloppily out of the tap, the sound amplified in the small space with its humid, pre-breathed air, its dim sour smell of gastric juices and sweat.

"Why me?" Emily blurts.

Lydia rinses the soap off her hands and wipes them once on the back pockets of her skirt.

"I didn't want my friends to know," Lydia says. "But I do appreciate it. I couldn't have done it on my own."

On her way out, Lydia squeezes Emily on the shoulder, her fingers, still damp, leaving splotched prints on Emily's silk blouse.

After Lydia is gone, Emily stays in the washroom and cries in big ugly gasps, mascara-thickened tears dribbling down her cheeks. She doesn't care if someone walks in. Let them. Let the whole office see her. The worst part of it is that Emily understands—even empathizes with—Lydia, who just wants to control the narrative of her life, to make it coherent and intelligible. And who doesn't want that?

They have so much in common.

The Emilies, who have been quiet all day, now chime in, tentatively, with slow reassuring voices.

"I feel sorry for her," Emily Brontë says.

"Imagine not being able to trust your friends with your secrets," Emily Dickinson says.

"What kind of a friendship is that?" Emily Davison says.

Emily, smiling a fragile smile, nods at the Emily in the mirror. "We tell each other everything."

LEAN INTO THE MIC

I.

"So high schools all take different approaches to sex ed. [*Lean into the mic.*] My school was the condom-on-the-banana-terrify-kids-so-that-they-think-they-could-contract-aids-from-a-wet-dream-or-from-a-lingering-wink variety. [*Left eye wink, right eye wink makes whole face wonky.*] Heavy on the pictures of oozing sores and pus-filled blisters fostering a general sense of dread and panic around sex. [*Pacing.*] Which makes everyone's first time so special. [*Stop pacing.*] I'm finally going to go all the way! And contract some horrible disease and transform into a ginormous slug, and I'll be forced to go to all the local high schools, a goopy mucus mess gooping behind me, and tell my sad-sack story [*lean into the mic*]—with the help of a retractable tentacle language interpreter—as a cautionary tale. Basically, if the sex ed at my high school was a movie genre [*lean into the mic*] it would be [*long beat*] horror."

People chuckled with one or two guffaws thrown in. I could hear each chair-adjustment creak and beer-gulping swallow. Up on that small stage I felt alive, converted into a viler, wilier, wilder version of myself. At parties I often stammered or bit my lip, uncertain of my role, but in this context I knew what was expected: people came to the open mic to hear people tell jokes or, more commonly, to hear themselves tell jokes.

I knew I wouldn't be the worst person there because a few people always bombed. At least I had some grasp of structure: setup, punchline, topper, callback. I'd taken classes and watched YouTube videos and Netflix specials. I threw myself into different voices. Laughter fortified my confidence and encouraged me to be bigger, bolder. I paced and stomped and curtsied.

When the clapping stopped, my anxiety surged. The room shrank. The stale smell of beer and bodies overwhelmed me. I hurried off-stage and beelined for the washroom, a tentative smile twisting my face. I didn't make eye contact with anyone because I was certain they'd give me a look swollen with pity or scorn. Two years of stand-up and still a wimp. I locked myself in a stall and performed deep breathing exercises, visualizing every inch of skin gulping restorative oxygen. *They laughed, right? For sure, for sure. They definitely laughed.*

I used to spend this time checking my Twitter feed, a zing of energy skipping through my blood when someone favourited or retweeted one of my tweets, but I'd deleted my account three months ago. Dopamine surges of social media approval couldn't counteract the added stress of seeing how many more followers other comedians had, how many more gigs and opportunities.

Calm enough to face any of the regulars who were still milling at the bar, I exited my chamber. One pint after a set is my rule. You never know who might want to talk to you or book you for a real gig. Most people had already wandered into the night, but along with a few older amateur comics—the ones who still made jokes about how women love shopping for shoes more than sucking dick—there was a skinny, curly brown-haired guy wearing a white T-shirt and black jeans, sitting by himself and sipping a glass of red wine.

I sat and ordered a beer.

"Slugs have astonishing sex lives. The Kama Sutra would be their kindergarten textbook." The guy, who I now saw was barely older than a teenager, angled his stool to face mine. "Leopard slugs swing from branches on self-created mucus rope like Cirque de Soleil silk aerialists, entwining themselves—caressing, devoted and present. Each lover both male and female, exchanging roles. It's very consensual and very hot."

"Good to know?" I glanced at the bartender to see if she was hearing what I was hearing, but she was at the other end of the room in a cloud of dishwasher steam. "Are you a biology student? An art student?"

"I'm just saying you might want to rethink that part of your set. If there were a sexually transmitted disease that could make me a slug, I would fuck everyone who'd consent to have me."

"Duly noted."

He chugged the rest of his wine, nodded at me and left.

As I walked home that night, weaving between troupes of stumbling drunk twenty-year-olds, I tried to parse that conversation, tried to decide whether I would spin it as funny or creepy when I told my husband Ben about it. I didn't think the guy had wanted to impress me with his comedic timing. Too earnest and spacy for that. Then again, maybe he was just a shitty joke-teller; most people were, most of the time I was.

And bringing up sex immediately was an aggressive move. A power play, one all women are used to, but this time it hadn't felt as icky or boring as it usually did. Maybe because of his young age? His ambiguous sexual orientation? Maybe because I'd found the slug sex description intriguing, even beautiful? Maybe because I hadn't considered changing anything about my set for months, for years, and the prospect both excited and terrified me.

I couldn't resolve my feelings about the encounter yet, so when my husband stirred from sleep and asked drowsily how my night went, I told him, *Fine, same old, same old, get some rest you have to wake up early for work*, then went to the living room and read everything I could find about slugs on the Internet.

II.

"You know what I always wanted though? [*Lean into the mic, long beat.*] One of those fake babies, one of those fake crying [*speed up and some pacing*], fake pooping mechanical ones you're supposed to carry around and care for over a week while you're trying to finish your calculus homework and go to swim practice, so you realize all on your own that you don't have the emotional maturity for a baby, and that—no duh [*throw hand in the air, casually*]—you should stay far, far away from penis or at least wrap it up. Anyway, I was asking my husband about whether or not they had these baby cockblockers at his school and he said, no way, they were an all-boys Catholic school and you absolutely didn't talk about sex, you just were not allowed to have it. [*Lean into the mic.*] I was like, um, you're not supposed to have sex with the babies!"

The reception to this joke depends, even more than normal, on audience intoxication. Drunk people love dirty jokes, even better if they involve babies, while sober people are more likely to temper their laughter based on cues from their friends or dates. Since it was only eight, the audience coughed and tittered politely, punctuated by a table-slapping cackle from my friend Janice, an investment banker and amateur Muay Thai fighter who attended my open mic sets at least once a month, often with a new gorgeous, Eastern European girlfriend in tow. Today she was alone, her muscular legs spread wide, treating herself to a pitcher of sangria.

As I progressed through my set, the lines, normally as instinctive as breathing, now felt angular and garish in my mouth. I stumbled self-consciously. How many times had Janice heard me say the exact same words in the exact same order? What was cute coming from someone in her twenties was surely contrived, try-hard, tragic even, coming from someone in her thirties.

Somehow I finished and headed to the washroom. My meditation retreat ended when Janice banged on the stall.

"Did you drown?"

I opened the door. She entered and slid the lock closed. From her purse she produced a baggie of cocaine and did a bump on the end of a shiny gold key before offering me some. I declined. Janice was confusing me for the younger me, the one who wrote all those jokes. She snorted a bit more.

"More people might have come if you'd tweeted about the show," she said.

"I deleted Twitter. Remember? Mental health, panic attacks, night terrors, et cetera."

"I thought you'd decided to be serious about this comedy thing."

"I am serious."

"Then Twitter would make sense, career-wise. I'm just saying."

"Thanks," I said, forcing a smile.

We headed to the bar area, Janice practically skipping, her pupils as large as billboard periods. The slug sex guy was there, wearing the same outfit and drinking the same wine. In this lighting, he resembled my high school boyfriend Dave, a devout Christian who'd begged and begged to watch me masturbate then broke up with me, disgusted, after I'd complied.

My throat was scratchy. My heartbeat whirred as though I'd received a contact coke high. Should I talk to him or ignore him?

Without noticing the shift in my mood, Janice led us to two seats directly beside slug-sex guy and proceeded to flirt with the bartender.

Filling my lungs with air, I tapped the man—boy, really, as he couldn't be over nineteen—on the shoulder.

"Banana slugs have been known to get their dicks stuck in slug snatches and then either he or his partner has to gnaw off the penis to free it." I'd rehearsed this fact this morning and I couldn't stop talking or I'd lose my momentum. Janice and the bartender and anyone within hearing distance focused their attention on me. "It's called apophallation. How does that affect your slutty gastropod theory?"

He drew back and stared at me with glazed, blank eyes.

"Sorry," he said in a meek voice. "I'm not sure..."

"What the fuck, Amanda?" Janice said. "And I thought I was the wasted one."

"Are you a comedian?" he said. "I'm new here. Probably just too stupid to get the joke. Sorry."

Janice put her hand on his shoulder and squeezed. He winced. "Apologies for my friend. She's off her meds."

"I thought... I must have mistaken you for..." My cheeks burned. I kept my eyes on the foam deflating atop my beer. "Excuse me."

Once in the washroom, I splashed cold water on my face. What happened out there? Was it the guy's twin brother? Was he blackout drunk last time? Was I just exhausted and confused? That could be it. I'd barely slept last night or the night before that or really since the last show. Still, that didn't explain it. Did it? Remembering the boy's soft, innocent voice, his genuine appearance of confusion sent new surges of embarrassment through my gut. I needed a distraction. I took the phone out of my bag and navigated to the Twitter home page but stopped myself at the last second.

Why should I care what other people thought of me anyway? I could be strong, an independent woman fearlessly spewing humour and truth into the world, bringing people together in a common emotional experience, freeing them from the compromises, privations and degradations of daily life. Or at least I could work toward being that kind of woman. I wished, not for the first time, that my stage persona could replace my weakling everyday identity.

Holding my head high, I returned to my friend at the bar. On the way there, the boy bumped into me and whispered, "Why don't you wear a wedding ring if you're married to Mr. Catholic School?"

"I lost it," I replied, rubbing the spot where, three years earlier, there would have been a modest silver band decorated with a diamond speck, a modest silver band that I'd forgotten in some gas station washroom, that could be in a pawn shop or at the bottom of a lake or on another person's finger by now. "And just never replaced it."

He smiled as though we both knew I was lying and he was indulging me, a soft papa spoiling his baby girl.

III.

"But seriously I recently had this pregnancy scare. My period was, like, [*long beat, lean into the mic*] three hours late. Whatever. I'm a hypochondriac. I realize pregnancy isn't a disease, but kinda, right? Anyway, so my period is late and I'm thinking, can I have this baby? [*Pacing.*] Like, are babies into whiskey and documentaries about climate change? Do they enjoy smoking weed and blasting Dolly Parton and dancing around the kitchen? Do they have insightful things to say about contemporary poetry? [*Long beat.*] Probably not. So, okay, that's one option down. So, can I have the baby and give it away? [*Speeding up.*] Like could I give the baby to some awesome queer couple who are these radical artists who make organic baby food from the heirloom beets they grow in their backyard and who will silkscreen the baby's onesie with mind-blowing quotes from Audre Lorde or Judith Butler and who will nurture that child and allow her to express herself? And she'll choose her own name and it'll be Glacier and Glacier'll live this wonderful, powerful little life full of creative fulfillment and wonder, and when she's fifteen [*speed up even more*], she'll reach out to me and we'll meet and she'll just think I'm so amazing and cool and she'll just praise me for how brave I was to give her away and, like, she'll be kinda obsessed with me and [*take a quick breath to emphasize how quickly you're talking*] I'll write an article about how devastating but vital the experience of giving away a child is and Glacier'll share the article through all the newest, hippest social media platforms and tweet about how great I am all the time and we'll do interviews together [*panting by now*] on all the podcasts and then I'll write a book and then a book is basically a movie deal and me and Glacier will be so so so so tight. [*Slow way way down, lean into the mic.*] But she won't need that much emotional support from me or that much money or anything because her parents are these, like, total earth goddesses."

"What do you think?" I asked Ben, who was sitting on the battered, plaid couch, various densely printed forms and contracts fanned on the coffee table in front of him. He worked long hours as a lawyer, which, combined with my nocturnal schedule, made finding couple time difficult.

"Did you change something?"

"Yes," I said, annoyed. "I told you I'm working on my material." Even though the old jokes felt stale, I wasn't ready to scrap everything and start over. "I added tons of details. The heirloom beets. The Audre Lorde. And I changed the name from Lemondrop to Glacier. More of a climate change edge this way. More realistic and political." I hated the way I talked about comedy sometimes, as though it were a noble calling and not a pathetic plea for external validation.

"Oh, right. An improvement, definitely."

"You didn't even listen. You're always distracted by your fucking work." I picked up a piece of paper only to realize it wasn't a contract at all but an energy bill—a pretty massive one.

He yanked it from my hand. "What do you want me to say? I've been supportive. Many women have utterly unsupportive partners, recklessly, cruelly unsupportive, but not me. You've been doing this ever since we got married. I've supported you, stayed silent and let you go on stage and tell all these lies about us."

"*Let* me? You let me? And I'm not telling lies. It's a character I play. My comedic alter-ego. People know the difference."

He gave me his *oh please, not everyone is from the big city and studied cultural theory* look.

"People who know comedy know the difference. And that's my audience. Those are my people."

"And they're more important to you than I am?"

"I could be telling way more personal jokes, you know."

"You'd have to write them."

That hurt. "No one wants to hear about a woman who can't have a baby. It's just sad."

We'd had this argument many times before, and at this point it usually fizzled—we're both more flighters than fighters—but this time Ben took several deep breaths, as though psyching himself up to continue. "It's not my choice to be sterile, you know." He fiddled with his hands. "You don't need to throw it in my face."

"I know that." His dejected expression softened me. "And it could be either of us. We won't know until the results come back." I realized then that we hadn't actually taken the tests yet. "Until we find the time to take the tests and the results come back." One more missing step, enough to create a comedy bit, anything to deflect from the real possibility that we'd never have kids and that without them our relationship would wither. "Until we get a referral to the right doctor and they take the tests and the results come back."

"I just—I just get the feeling it's me."

I rubbed his elbow. "Eighteen months isn't long, isn't any-thing. We actually have to be awake at the same time to have the baby-making sex. You're always at work."

The word *sex* switched him on. He grabbed a belt loop in my jeans and pulled me toward him. "Someone has to pay the bills."

"Speaking of which..." I wriggled free of his embrace and rum-maged through the papers for the energy bill from earlier, but he slapped my hand—like a child or dog still learning not to play rough—and began sorting everything into piles.

"They're in a very specific order," he said.

"I think you have a bill mixed in somewhere..."

"When did you decide to reactivate your Twitter account?"

I stopped my investigation. "What are you taking about? You know I deleted my account three months ago."

He opened his laptop and showed me my profile, which fea-tured a blurry—and many chinned—picture of me standing in front of a microphone and a bio that read *Amanda Hunt tells jokes at open mics around town.*

"Look," Ben said.

Panicking and confused, I scanned the tweets. Was I the victim of a hoax, an identity theft, a character assassination? As I read, my heart rate settled. The tweets were mostly just announcements about upcoming shows, jokes from my set and some Amy Schu-mer retweets. A boring, neutered rendering of my personality, but not malevolent. It occurred to me it might be fan-made, and I was touched. Then I clicked around some more. I was following fifty people—all D-list celebrities, plus Janice. Twenty-five followers, a full hundred less than my previous account. Embarrassing. Who was follower number one? Surprise, surprise: Janice.

"Janice," I said. "What the fuck?"

I was going to call her when I noticed a familiar face. He wore a collared blue shirt instead of his usual white T-shirt and his face had the bland confidence of a mediocre accountant rather than the timid yet smirky arrogance of a schoolboy, but it was him. I was sure. His name, supposedly, was Greg Shape, and his handle was @greatshape, a choice so inane it teetered on brilliance. A joke like that—assuming it was a joke—lived or died by delivery. I went to his profile. His last three tweets were all retweets of my feed—my fake feed, fan feed, friend feed, I didn't know what to call it. I imagined him clicking the retweet icon. I imagined him clicking while sitting cross-legged on a mattress in his apartment—a shitty basement place with roaches, the kind you can only tolerate when you're young. I imagined him clicking with one hand and stroking himself with the other.

"Why would Janice do that?" Ben asked, leaning over to look at the screen. "And who is Greg?"

I closed the computer and wrapped my arms around his neck. "Shall we try again?"

IV.

"And then I'm thinking like, no, this is ridiculous, I don't want to get stretch marks and not drink or do mushrooms for nine months [*left eye wink*] and shove an [*lean into mic*] alien out my vagina and have it be all stretched and busted up and shit. And then I'm thinking: I'll have an abortion. It will be this really empowering moment because I'll finally be able to prove how pro-choice I am, and I'll gather all my female friends around me and we'll be so open with each other and they'll support me and it will be this bonding experience. And then I'll get the abortion and it will be kinda sad and tough but I'll feel totally calm about how it was the right choice. And I'll talk to some pro-life people and I'll be so authentic and moving when I describe my experience that I'll change their minds. It'll turn into this huge movement [*gesture with arms, but don't drop mic!!*] and people will be like, oh yeah, why do I care so much about what women do with their uteruses? [*Speed up.*] And the fetus billboard industry will collapse, and I'll write all these articles and they'll go viral, and then it's [*singsongy voice, maybe actually hop?*] hop-skip-jump: book. [*Again, louder.*] Hop-skip-jump: movie deal. And I'll be this feminist icon [*speed up*] talking on panels and I'll be so radically vulnerable, and people will be obsessed with me and they'll tweet about me and praise me but they won't need much from me emotionally or financially because they have other people for that! [*Lean into the mic.*] You know?"

I knew I was rushing, bulldozing through the pauses, the cracks in logic that gestured for the audience to enter the demented, silly, self-involved world I'd created, a world that seemed increasingly remote. But I had to keep talking or I was going to panic. Greg was in the corner, sitting at the table next to Ben, who was sitting with Janice. All of them in one room, watching me screw up.

After some lacklustre applause, I joined Janice and my husband at the bar. Greg, absorbed in his wine, was perched on the other side of the room. Seeing Janice and Ben together disoriented me. It seemed imperative to keep all three of these people as far apart as possible. It was as though my favourite characters from different television shows had appeared in the same crossover episode. I didn't want them to interact, to wrestle for dominance, one reality gobbling the others. Or maybe *I* was a character in several different television shows and my personality had begun to migrate, become fluid. I worried I would use my reverent and earnest drama voice in a slapstick comedy or my husky femme fatale voice in a sexless mother-of-the-tween-idol role.

I pecked Ben on the cheek and asked him to order me a beer before dragging Janice to the washroom. "Twitter," I said.

"I thought we discussed this." Janice bristled, launching straight into self-defence, assuming, no doubt, that although I'd been calm when I'd first confronted her, I had worked myself into a fury and was now going to berate her. "I said I'd take it down after a week if you still wanted me to get rid of it. I told you what that brand manager said. I sent you that article. How vital—"

"I've thought about it," I said. "I think you're right. I need it for my career."

Janice nodded, surprised. "Great," she said, drawing out the word and examining my demeanour for any potential booby traps. Finding none, she continued. "Great, that's great. The password is Glacier."

"Glacier?"

She smiled. "Much better than Lemondrop."

I reached for my phone and signed in. Notifications! Retweets and followers and likes! Why had I ever deprived myself?

"What does Ben think about the return to social media?"

I shrugged, clicking and clicking.

"I guess he has other things to worry about," Janice said. "Why didn't you tell me he lost his job? I had to hear it from one of the partners at his firm. This bombshell, a Tippi Hedren bottle blonde I went on a date with last night named Maya something. Do you know her? Anyway, it's nothing to be ashamed of. Not in this economy."

All the muscles in my body slackened. Chills scurried over my skin. I sat on the toilet and ran my hands through my hair.

"Two months ago?" Janice said.

I stared at her, remembering the mystery bill.

"I'm sure he was going to tell you," Janice said. "Shit! You really didn't know?"

"He's been going to work every day," I whispered. "Wearing his suit and everything."

"I don't know what to say…"

I stood up. "Do you have any coke?"

"Is that the best idea?" Janice said. "Shouldn't we discuss, debate, express our feelings?"

"Nope," I said. "Coke, coke and more coke."

All my insecurities melted away as I returned to the bar, soaring high, the back of my throat coated in chemicals. I ignored Ben, who had been cornered by one of the regular comics, a name-dropping woman with aggressive cleavage, and floated over to Greg.

"Washroom," I said. "Now."

He grinned at me as though he'd been expecting this, then chugged his wine.

Not even the beads of piss speckling the seat and the faint iron smell emanating from the silver bin could dampen my excitement. Nor could the prospect of someone walking in. Let Ben in. Let Janice in. Give me an audience. I didn't give a fuck.

"I can't create a rope of mucus for us to swing on," I said. "But I can pretend to be a slug." I pressed my hands into my thighs and undulated my body, a vertical snake dance.

Yanking my hair, he pushed me against the metal wall. With his face so close to mine, I could see faint wrinkles by his eyes.

The sex was swift and vaguely painful. Maybe the drugs had desensitized me, but I couldn't feel much and had the sensation of drifting above my body. He didn't even attempt to touch my clit, so I tried to help myself. It was over so quickly.

As he was doing up his jeans, I asked, "How was it?"

"Same as usual," he said.

The stall door banged shut behind him. The taps blasted. Soap plopped stickily from a dispenser. I tried to assess the situation, to perform an inventory of my bodily and emotional reactions. Was I surprised? Ashamed? I didn't know. If I had to choose an adjective to describe my mood at that moment it would be *awake*. My pants still around my ankles, I went on Twitter and stalked through the people Greg followed. Marisa, Iffah, Ariana, Kim: female comedians, all of them. It was so obvious. I laughed and laughed and deleted my account.

V.

"And so I go into the washroom and there's blood on my underwear and for a minute I'm super bummed. [*Long beat, lean into the mic.*] Like not about the underwear, those were already covered in a decades-worth of period stains. [*Lean into the mic.*] I'm just bummed because I was *this* close [*demonstrate with fingers*] to being super famous. [*Lean into the mic.*] But at least now I don't have to feel guilty or weird or anything but super-duper pumped about how much coke I just snorted. You know?"

I forced myself to tell all the old jokes one last time, to give them a proper burial before the final punchline. A punchline is a revelation, a conversion. It alters everything that came before it, tripping the audience and forcing them to balance in a new reality. But it can also be cruel and stubborn, over-determining the meaning of a story.

Two months after I removed Twitter and Ben from my life, I went to the washroom, as usual. Did my breathing exercises, as usual. But unlike Comedy Amanda, Everyday Amanda didn't have any blood on her underwear, and if the two vertical lines ignited by her urine that morning were to be believed, there wouldn't be any again for many months. And here's the thing, the sucker punchline: I was happy, relieved. Ready.

CONSTANT WEIGHT
WITHOUT FINS

W hat scared Alison most about freediving was how easy it was. How easy to let the air drain from her lungs and limbs, how easy to revert to a pre-mammalian state, to imagine herself as an eel undulating in the dark chill, a ruffle of gills behind her ears. At times she worried that this comfort at three hundred feet below land proved what she'd always suspected: she was a holdover from a more primitive design. Not quite human.

Alison sat cross-legged on a limestone ledge overlooking Dean's Blue Hole, a walled depression that plunged over seven hundred feet down and that revealed itself at the surface as a circle of indigo water surrounded by turquoise shallows. On a leather cord around her neck hung the sinkhole's likeness: azure glass with a blob of navy in the middle. She'd bought the necklace online while recovering from a hysterectomy. It was an affirmation of her commitment to the sport. She held the pendant as she inhaled and exhaled, her waist contracting to twenty inches and expanding to twenty-four.

Ten days.

Ten days left to embrace her animal otherness, to dive without anxiety, without oxygen-huffing emotions. She would micromanage every element of her body, destroying the distinction between conscious and unconscious control. No enzyme would be secreted, no blood cell deployed without her permission.

In ten days, she would attempt to break the female world record of sixty-seven metres currently held by Ashley Chapman. Alison competed in various freediving disciplines, but she loved Constant Weight Without Fins best because it was the purest. Unlike Variable Weight, Free Immersion and No Limits, there were no propulsion equipment or weights used. It was just her body, unadorned, slicing its way into the airless depths.

Alison hadn't always been so concerned about purity. Years ago, when she'd first gotten serious about diving, she'd allowed her training partner and then-boyfriend Tony to inject her with something he called The Attack, a mixture of vitamin D and great white shark sperm, which he purchased from a Laotian acupuncturist. He claimed it would make her a more fearless diver, but she never noticed any real difference. She only went along with it because Tony was her first boyfriend, and back then the shots were the highlight of her week.

Every Thursday night after practice, they'd have a light dinner of grilled salmon salad dressed with balsamic vinaigrette. For dessert, a few squares of dark chocolate. Afterward they'd go into the bedroom and Tony would prepare the syringe while she changed into a peach silk nightgown. He'd dim the lights, then drape her across his lap and fold back her skirt like a parent about to deliver a spanking. He'd give her the needle, which stung a bit but in a sexy way, and he would kiss the injection site delicately before easing her onto the floor and making love to her from behind, her knees and palms cool and supported against the wood floor. Neither spoke the whole time. They both knew what to expect and what was expected of them.

These date nights weren't enough to save the relationship, though. Alison began to tire of Tony's ambition. She felt as though he considered himself to be the only real diver in the relationship, and once or twice she even found herself thinking the same. So to maintain her focus, she broke it off. Six months later she was handed a diagnosis of ovarian cancer. When Alison confessed about The Attack and the Laotian acupuncturist to the doctor, he mumbled something about quackery and then assured her that there was probably no link and even if there were she should focus on getting better. Even so, she'd always believed the cancer was a punishment for allowing Tony to contaminate her.

Bleached grass tickled Alison's feet as she continued her morning meditation and breathing exercises. The air was fresh, tinged with salt. The Bahaman sun wasn't yet high in the sky, and its warmth was as soothing as amniotic fluid. She was confident that she could make it past sixty-seven metres. Going down had never been her problem. It was forcing herself back up and turning away from that giddy freedom that was difficult.

The International Association for the Development of Apnea's rules stipulated that when divers resurfaced they had to execute three tasks in order: remove their goggles, make a circle with their thumb and index finger, and say, "I'm okay." If divers messed up, forgetting one item or doing them in the wrong sequence, their dive would be invalidated. The reasoning was that divers had to prove they were consciously aware, that both body and mind had returned from the underworld. Alison thought of this ritual as a cleansing spell, a reassurance to audience and judge that the divers hadn't been transformed by their superhuman feats. She'd been disqualified in the past for failing to perform the sacred sequence.

Back in her cabin Alison sat in front of her laptop. On Tuesdays she had a long-standing Skype appointment with her parents. They were sitting side by side, partially obstructing the Chagall print on the white wall behind them—a wonky blue town with a workman angel floating above the peaked roofs. They filled her in on their retired life, discussing their various health problems and recipes involving sea bass and ancient grains. She told them about the weather and the conch fritters the cook had made for her and the team. They didn't discuss the upcoming dive or their flight to the Bahamas or anything else related to the true substance of her existence. She'd written them an email banning these topics from their conversations, and so far her parents had obliged. Talking about things, Alison believed, could diminish their power.

Just as they were saying their goodbyes, her mother interrupted.

"Have you spoken to your sister recently?" she said.

"I'm talking to her Sunday," Alison said.

"I actually liked that guy," her father said. "Good taste in music."

"Poor girl," her mother said. "She's really upset. She hasn't said anything exactly, but I can just tell. She's so sensitive."

Alison tapped her foot against the floor, told her blood to cool. "I already said I'm talking to Brianna on Sunday."

"We never have to worry about you, Ali," her mother said. Alison stopped herself from pointing out that freediving was among the most dangerous sports in the world.

Most of the time Alison liked to train alone, but she couldn't do everything by herself. On Wednesday she had dinner with her seven teammates, the people who would set up the rope and attach tags identifying the depth along the way. Alison would have to carry one of these back to the surface and show it to the judges to prove she'd been there. Her team would also pilot the boat and some members would scuba dive partway down with her and accompany her on the last hundred feet of her ascent, the part where hydrogen narcosis or blackout was most likely to occur.

They called themselves Alison's pod, a nickname Alison herself never used.

For dinner they had fish chowder, broiled grouper and papaya salad prepared by their cook. Alison didn't eat any of the chowder. She had a few bites of grouper and a thin slice of papaya, the sweetness explosive on her tongue. She smiled nervously as the conversation swirled around her. She removed a sliver of bone from between her teeth and placed it on her plate parallel to the knife. She never knew what to say to these people her age who had children and spouses and friends. Who were skilled divers, but not exceptional ones. They laughed and gulped down creamy spoonfuls of chowder, gossiping about other freedivers and speculating on which judges the Association would send. Alison wanted to be alone. One of her teammates, Doug, put his arm around her shoulder, and drew her close. "You don't have to speak now, pod-queen. Just don't forget those magic words."

In unison, the table erupted: "I'm okay!"

On Sunday she spoke to her sister Brianna over Skype. Brianna was sitting on her balcony in a pink terry cloth robe and sipping something bubbly and orange out of a champagne flute. The green and blue glass of condo buildings rose in clumps in the background, like millions of aquariums stacked on top of each other.

"What are you drinking there?" Alison was determined to keep the conversation light.

"It's not like I'm keeping it," Brianna said, taking a defiantly long swig.

"That's not what I meant."

"Well, it's not a *Jaws* jizz injection, but it keeps me afloat."

Clenching her teeth, Alison ordered her pulse to steady. "Thanks for that. Makes me super happy I told you."

"Jesus." Brianna opened her eyes wide. "Touchy. I thought you were over that. You know I was telling this guy at work the other day about freediving. He thought it was just the most hilarious thing he'd ever heard."

"Great." Alison reached for the mouse.

"Stop," Brianna said. "I'm sorry, I'm sorry. I'm a total hormone-a-thon these days."

"Well, I'm sorry, too, but I can't talk to you like this. It's too close. Everything."

"Is this about the email you sent?" Brianna put down her glass and started talking in a high voice, the one she used for all her imitations, while bouncing her head back and forth and rolling her eyes. "Dear family. Please respect my wishes not to talk about anything ever and to lord my prissy ass over every one of you."

Alison exhaled and inhaled deeply through her nostrils. "I really am going now." The cursor floated above the red icon of a phone.

"I'm just so pissed at you, okay?" Brianna said. "I mean, I get the whole dive or whatever. But I want you here with me. I need you here."

Alison took her hand off the mouse. "You'll be fine, Brie," she said. "If it makes you feel any better, the pain during my surgery was pretty minimal."

Alison looked back on the day of surgery almost fondly. The pleasing crinkly sound her gown had made, how firm and official the table had felt beneath her back. It was so nice of everyone, the nurses and the doctors, to restore her body. Best of all there had been the familiar buoyant sensation as the anesthesia seeped into her blood while she counted down, down, down.

"But I'm not you, Ali." Brianna leaned back into her chair and retrieved her glass. "And they're not removing a tumour."

Alison clicked hard. Brianna vanished.

Alison had always believed that Brianna could have been a better diver than her if she'd stuck with it. When they were younger they used to take turns seeing who could swim farther underwater in the local pool. The lifeguards would beg them to stop, blasting their whistles and waving their arms, but they kept pushing themselves. At seven, Alison could do one and a half laps, but Brianna, a year older, could manage two, sometimes two and a half. If there were boys watching, she would even do a little corkscrew turn at the end to show off. But it was never important to her. Alison used to fantasize that they were mermaids separated from their true parents at birth, their sparkly rainbow tails slashed into ordinary human legs.

The night before the dive, Alison had a meeting with her team. They went over the next day's schedule one last time and reviewed safety procedures. Everyone seemed excited and tense. To protect herself from this spiky energy, Alison envisioned being surrounded by a force field. She was grateful to her teammates, she truly was, but she had to keep herself apart from them if she was going to succeed. She told herself the diving record would justify her coldness. If you could accomplish something like that, people didn't expect you to act normally. In fact, they were disappointed if you did.

After they disbanded, Alison was walking along the beach on the way back to her hut when she heard the sound of someone jogging behind her. Doug.

"Can I walk you home?" he asked.

Alison sighed and nodded. They walked without speaking for a while, admiring the stars. At least he knew how to be comfortable with silence.

About two hundred feet from her cabin, Doug reached his hand under the back of her shirt and rubbed her spine. She jerked sideways, swatting his hand away.

"What the hell?" she said.

"Just checking," he said.

"For what? Scoliosis?"

"A dorsal fin."

Alison stiffened and turned away. "I don't know what you mean."

"Sure you don't," he said and hugged her, lifting her into the air and humming the theme from *Jaws* as he spun her around. "Shark Woman!"

He put her down and she blinked tears out of her eyes.

"Hey," he said. "Hey, there, relax. No one's judging you. I'm buds with Tony from way back. He never talked about me?"

Alison shook her head no.

"He was always trying to get me to try that shit, The Attack or whatever he calls it, bragging about how he had a connection with a heavy duty Laotian shaman and how it would make me tap into my true predator instincts. But I don't like jabbing stuff in my butt."

Alison was stunned. She'd always believed that The Attack was something she alone shared with Tony, something that only existed in the separate dimension created by their unique relationship. She tried to walk away but Doug had her by the arm.

"I don't know what Tony told you," she said, "but I haven't in years and years."

"Since the cancer," he said softly.

"Fuck off," Alison jerked herself free of his grip.

"We're just sharing here." He grabbed both her elbows and spoke so close to her that she could smell the whey protein powder on his breath. "No need for that kind of language."

Doug kissed her, prying her lips apart with his thick, wet tongue. Alison closed her eyes and prayed adrenalin would stop surging through her veins and destabilizing her inner ecosystem. He clasped her tighter.

"Don't be so stiff, baby," he said. "It'll help you relax."

Alison considered hitting him, but who knew what he'd do. Punch her. Break her collarbone. Anxiety was the worst pollutant there was. It was best to just go limp.

Doug fondled her breasts and rubbed his crotch against hers. He reached down her shorts. "Come on. It's not like you can get pregnant."

Alison kneed him in the groin and he shoved her hard, sending her flying into the sand. She stood up and brushed the grains off her shirt and shorts.

"Whatever," Doug said. "You were bone dry. Not that I should be surprised."

Alison didn't say anything. Doug stared at her for a few moments, shaking his head. He sighed and walked away.

Once he was out of sight, Alison began to head home with deliberate slowness, instructing herself to relax.

When she got to her cabin she took a shower, turning the water as hot as she could stand and then even hotter. Lathering her neck, she realized that her necklace was gone. She stumbled out of the shower and, covered in foam, searched through her heap of clothes. Nothing. Tomorrow, then. She rinsed and dried off before pulling on an oversized T-shirt with a picture of a palm tree on it. As she climbed into bed, she took several big breaths and tried to imagine herself as a jellyfish glowing in the darkness, glowing a clean white light.

Searching for the pendant along the beach she encountered swirls of seaweed like clumps of mermaid hair that had been yanked from scalps. It was dawn and light crept in a line across the horizon, turning the grey light golden. Her parents were probably collecting their luggage in Nassau now or checking into their hotel. They'd agreed to meet after the dive, as Alison had requested. They always respected her instructions, even when they shouldn't have.

She couldn't find the necklace anywhere, and after an hour of looking, she accepted that she would have to dive without it. She hated any change of routine, but she couldn't afford to freak out over it. There wasn't enough time.

The rest of the morning went as planned. A light jog, breathing exercises, meditation. From her perch above Dean's Blue Hole, she could see the team setting up the rope with its assortment of tags glittering like fishing lures. Doug waved at her and she shut her eyes, exhaling and inhaling. Sixty-seven and a half metres. Sixty-seven and a half metres.

It was nothing.

As the morning wore on, people began to gather by the water's edge. Some benches had been set up for the audience. She saw her parents wearing their matching Tilley hats and khaki shorts. Were they nervous or excited? Would they be here if Brianna had told them the truth about the abortion? She wished her sister were with them instead of in a waiting room somewhere. She wished she were with her sister, holding her hand or brushing her hair. She wished that none of them were there, that none of them even knew about the dive.

Alison saw two judges walk toward the beach and then one of the teammates gave her the signal to come down to the water's edge. The water was warm and clear, and the boat wobbled slightly as she climbed aboard. She looked over the edge of the boat to avoid making eye contact with Doug. The water went from turquoise to indigo. They anchored the boat and she adjusted her goggles. She slipped into the water and floated on her back beside the rope, gulping air into her lungs. A judge counted down from five to one. Alison flipped over and dove. She pulled water around her, parting it to make way for her body. The world got colder and darker and more familiar. She could sense the rope beside her. She could see the tag for sixty-seven and a half metres just ahead. It was bigger than the rest but she didn't grab it. She kept kicking and kicking until she couldn't see the rope, her legs so smoothly coordinated it was as though they were fused together.

LOVE LASTS FOREVER BUT
A TATTOO LASTS LONGER

No perky carnations enlivened the institutional orange and beige decor, no flower girl flounced down the aisle or ran shyly into her mother's arms, no organist cracked his knuckles and poised his supple fingers above brass knobs. The wedding lasted five minutes. It took place in a Clorox-perfumed alcove off the prison visitation room and the wedding cake was a Baby Ruth from the vending machine. The priest smelled of hot dogs, relish speckled like radioactive jizz in his moustache. He resembled a wax Jeff Goldblum that had been left all day in the sun, his features lopsided, the right side of his mouth drooping and his left ear lobe flapping against a ruddy neck. Eyes closed, he stumbled through the ceremony, his voice veering between volumes as if controlled by a remote being passed back and forth between a person suffering from a migraine and someone's elderly, hard-of-hearing aunt.

I didn't give a shit. All I cared about was Jake. Jake with his shaved head and chapped lips, his bushy eyebrows and expressive nostrils. He was making goofy faces at me, tongue darting, eyes flaring and crossing. Idiot that I was, I was misty-eyed; my heart boomed with happiness. As requested, I was wearing a white dress with a neon pink push-up bra and pantie set flashing through the sheer, itchy fabric. Before Jake kissed me, he grinned and took a step back, admiring the words TOGETHERCOLOURED INSTANT tattooed in Helvetica across my chest, the black ink, mixed with Bing Crosby III's ashes, raised and scabbed. Jake told me he'd fallen in love with me the first time I read e.e. cummings, his favourite poet, to Line Break, a poetry group that I used to run at the penitentiary.

After we said our I dos, we signed the marriage certificate with two sullen guards serving as last-minute witnesses. Jake's brother Jordan had cancelled the night before, claiming food poisoning. My mother had refused to come because when she'd voiced her concerns about the marriage, I had responded like the smug bitch I was back then: I told her she was just jealous. "Unlike you, I'll actually have a husband who doesn't run around on me," I'd said. "I'll know where he is every second."

I didn't even notice Jake during my first Line Break session. Then again, I was nervous that the men gathered in a semi-circle around me were just biceps and goatees and macho energy. My skin was gauzy with sweat—after hearing about the program, my mother insisted that I wear a thick black turtleneck, baggy jeans and running shoes despite the fact that it was August. She didn't want me to "inflame the poor fellows' desires" by wearing my "usual pin-up girl getups."

A half-remembered poetry pep talk I'd been practising on my way there stuttered out of my mouth as the prisoners nodded encouragingly, as though I was a six-year-old butchering a violin solo at the local talent show. I had them write a poem using the words *free* and *mellifluous*. The second word—so utterly pretentious and wrongheaded, I find it almost sweet now—took on a staggering number of meanings, from a monster with a musical anus to a type of bright yellow hallucinogenic wine. In my youth

and stupidity, I assumed the inmates didn't know the true meaning of the word, but I would later learn they'd been fucking with
me—I wasn't the first Line Break graduate student they had
encountered, and I wouldn't be the last.

Still, I must have done something right because the next day
my carrel at the library was full of tulips and hyacinths, and there
was a card from Jake that read, *To the girl with the mellifluous voice,
please free us from bullshit words like mellifluous. –Jake. P.S. Do you
always dress like Steve Jobs?* I couldn't figure out how he had managed to contact a florist from prison until six months later when
Jordan told me Jake always called him to arrange flowers.

"Always, as in once? For me?" I'd said.

"Sure," Jordan said and smiled.

Jordan was a tattoo artist specializing in morbid ink, the quasi-legal
practice of mixing ink with ashes, a person's or a pet's, as part of
a memorial tattoo. He would only do them for friends of friends
because he was worried inspectors would start to crack down on it
if the practice became widely known. Jordan was certain it was safe.

"Carbon in the ink," he said. "Carbon in the ashes. What's the
difference?"

Still deluded enough to think of myself as a poet, I wrote several pieces on the subject with lines like "The skin white as the
pearly gates./ Death inside./ Outside./ Forever." I would read
them to Jordan, who was nice enough to only smirk a little. "Love
lasts forever but a tattoo lasts longer," he would say by way of cri-
tique. I'd been hanging out with Jordan a lot. Nobody else would
let me talk freely about Jake; nobody else took our relationship
seriously.

"Did you ever notice that Jake's right eye is a slightly more
intense blue than his left eye?" I would say as he sterilized his nee-
dles or arranged the sheets of Donald Duck and Chinese character flashes in the window.

"Isn't it sweet how Jake always mixes up *their* and *there,* and *you're* and *your*?"

Jordan never commented one way or the other, but sometimes we would get a beer at the Drunken Mermaid after work and he would tell stories about Jake: how as boys they would hold such intense Monopoly games that one time they both got bladder infections from holding their piss in for so long, neither wanting to go to the bathroom and risk the other one cheating, or how they would get their father to tell his alien abduction story whenever they wanted to avoid chores. When Jordan recounted stories about high school parties and double dates, I would crack peanut shells loudly and gnash the salty flesh until he stopped.

Other people expressed either derision (my friends) or concern (my mother) about my relationship with Jake. Worst of all were the students in my workshops who thought I was making him up to get attention, to set myself apart and brand myself as an outlaw poet. I didn't realize it at the time, but I should have nurtured this idea. Maybe then my supervisor wouldn't have thought I was getting "too involved" and yanked me from the Line Break program.

I'd initially met Jordan after Jake asked me to take care of his boxer, Bing Crosby II. He said he didn't believe that Jordan took his duties sufficiently seriously. "I think he's giving him No Name dog food," he said. "All anuses and spleens and snouts."

I texted Jordan and he told me to meet him at the tattoo shop. Bing Crosby II was tied to a bike rack outside, tugging furiously on the leash. When I tried to pet him he barked this weird whiny bark that I can only describe as a mix between a foghorn and a didgeridoo.

From inside the shop, I could hear someone laughing.

Jordan came outside and shook my hand. He looked like Jake, same bald head and full lips, only scrawnier and with more tattoos.

"He's beautiful," I said.

"Inbred as fuck," Jordan said. "I don't know why my brother insisted on getting a thoroughbred. That's some eugenics shit if you ask me."

"You know Jake," I said and giggled. I wanted to get out of there, but I also wanted Jordan to tell his brother how hot and cool I was—why else would I have spent all morning deciding between a black dress with white polka dots and a white dress with black polka dots?

Jordan nodded. "You free later? Want to grab a beer?"

"Not today," I said, a little taken aback. I didn't want to give the impression that I was interested in him romantically. "Maybe I could come by with coffee tomorrow?"

"Sure." Jordan untied the dog and handed the leash to me. "Decaf soy latte, please."

The idea of having Jake's dog, a being he'd potty trained and play-fought with and petted, thrilled me. I spent hours preparing steak and sweet potato for him on his first night, imagining the day when I would get to cook for Jake. But the thrill soon wore off with Bing Crosby II flailing through the apartment, his thick nails gouging the hardwood as he pissed and shat and impregnated my shitsu-poodle mix, Stanza. I forgave him when their progeny, Bing Crosby III, was born. The puppy was truly hideous with oversized paws, a limp pompadour and a stunted fluffy tail that almost looked like a rabbit's but I loved him because he was a herald of the babies Jake and I would have. "Our beautiful son," I wrote on the back of the photos I brought to Jake in prison. When Bing Crosby III was killed in a tragic car accident, I had him cremated, using some of the ashes for myself and saving some for Jake when he got out.

When I was feeling frustrated about our situation, I liked to imagine myself taking care of Jake as a little boy, how we would play in the bath for hours building castles out of green apple-scented bubbles and drowning his rubber ducky and staging complex naval battles, his little wrinkled body secure in the claw-foot tub. I liked to imagine pushing him on a swing, high enough to freak him out a bit so he cowered in my arms afterward. I liked to imagine soothing him, ruffling his hair and rubbing his back, after a crushing Little League defeat. I liked to imagine daubing rubbing alcohol on a scraped knee, his whole body wincing against the sting. Best of all I liked to imagine sending him to his room without supper as punishment for some minor infraction—a broken lamp or a pinched cousin—and locking the door, knowing he was inside, a tantrum in Batman pajamas wailing against the injustice of the universe.

Although she liked to protest, my mother was secretly pleased by the relationship. It gave her an excuse to call me all the time.

"Any news about Jake's parole?"

"Nope," I said, though in truth his lawyer had been flooding my inbox with messages on the subject.

"I saw your father." Talking about my father was the real reason she wanted to call me.

"On route 123 or on the side of a bus?" I balanced the phone in the crook of my neck, propped my feet against the kitchen table and began painting my toenails red.

"His face was in my mailbox." My mother was probably sitting in her living room, stroking one of her cats or else in the kitchen staring out at the clouds.

"I hope you threw him out."

Nothing.

I put down the bottle of polish. "Seriously, mother."

"Fine, fine," she said. "Have you spoken to him recently?"

"Did you look at the websites I sent you?"

"Online dating is for pervs and sad lonely people."

My toenails gleamed. I blew on them to speed up the drying process. "Perfect for a hardcore masochist."

"That isn't funny. Talk sense. When are you coming to visit me?" My mother lived with two Persian cats who sashayed through her one-bedroom apartment like glam-rock stars from the eighties, swishing their fabulous tails, purring a steady synth bassline and cocking their squished faces with haughty flair. I hated visiting her because I would leave covered in long white hairs too stubborn to be defeated by any lint roller.

"Soon, Mom. I promise. But you have to promise to throw Dad out."

"Fine."

My father had cheated on her for many years, and after a brief attempt at an open marriage—one that ended with my mother dressed in head scarf and shades bawling in a movie theatre as she spied on Dad feeding his date a Swedish berry— they finally split up when I was five. My father quickly remarried. His second wife Lola was a financial planner who favoured hot pink caftans and hub cap-sized gold studs. She was loud and crass and always had a menthol in hand. At first I liked how outspoken and strong she seemed, so different from my sensitive mother. But as I got older, I started to regard her as tacky, especially after my father's new ad campaign, which, I was convinced, was entirely her fault. I will never forget the first time I saw the park bench with his face on it. His bleached teeth and rusty skin and cowboy squint. "Been in an accident?" The sign read. "Call Leonard Martin at 1 800 CAR HIT U." The ad was infuriating for many reasons, not the least of which was that it made no sense. Shouldn't it have been "CAR HIT ME?" Whenever someone at school insulted the ad, I laughed along with everyone else. I laughed at the penises and cigars and speech bubbles that attached themselves to his mouth. My father and I spoke less and less, and then not at all.

Jake was two years into an eight-year sentence when I met him. He seemed incapable of talking about his crime seriously, not that he didn't love to talk about it; he did. Sometimes it involved duffle

bags of cash and a beautiful, harelipped Yakuza hit dame named
Princess Marigold, sometimes black-market firecrackers that
exploded into an expression of the lighter's darkest fear and once,
a recalcitrant getaway camel. I never knew what to make of it but
because he'd assured me that he never hurt or killed or sexually
molested anyone, I let it go. A month before the wedding Jordan
finally admitted, late one night after having tattooed a rose full
of Aunt Rose's ashes onto a young woman's thigh, that Jake was
in for dealing pot and mushrooms, a "fuckload of pot and mushrooms" according to Jordan, from his dorm room. I was grateful
both because the banal nature of Jake's crime made him more palatable to my mother and because it made him less palatable to
the hordes of inmate lovers who stalked the Internet searching for
their death-row Prince Charming.

I know I should have felt a kinship with the other women visiting their husbands, the women I waited in line with on Tuesday
afternoons, the women who wore wedge heels and tiny dresses
with push-up bras, their hair blow-dried, their eyeliner and lip
liner perfect and their nails freshly adhered, but I didn't. I was an
asshole. I didn't believe Jake was like the other convicts, and by
extension, I didn't think I was like the other wives. Most of the visits happened in the waiting room, which was always crackling with
energy. Jake would tell me about the guards' shenanigans and gossip about the other inmates. He didn't like to talk about himself
unless it was to discuss a trip we would take together when he got
out. "We'll scuba dive in Australia and horseback ride in Argen-
tina," he'd say. "We'll ski in Austria and surf in Antarctica. The only
real country is a country that starts with A in my opinion."

We were allowed conjugal visits four times a year on the condition that Jake had been behaving himself. They took place in
a nearby apartment full of white furniture made from particle
board. The prison provided scratchy towels, discount condoms
and thin wedges of yellow soap. They wouldn't let me bring my

own. A guard stood outside but we didn't let that stop us from enjoying ourselves—looking back, it probably increased my enjoyment knowing Jake was stuck in there with me. I loved stripping for him and revealing my new tats: a tulip travelling up my shin, the letter J in courier beside the bright blue veins in my wrist. I loved washing him afterward, lathering the soap against his skin, his arms limp by his sides.

After the wedding, I dropped out of grad school. The passive-aggressive workshops and love triangles just didn't seem to matter anymore. My mother was relieved and suggested I do something practical like go to nursing school or write a sensational memoir about being married to a convict, preferably "something Opera Winfrey or HBO would appreciate." Instead I became an apprentice at Jordan's tattoo studio. I practised inking grapefruits and oranges with stars and hearts, then with busty ladies and barbed wire and Celtic knots. On my own thighs I wrote out stanzas from Sylvia Plath and Anne Sexton, each letter a different colour and font. Jordan was a patient teacher and my skill set became solid but never inspired. I could do any of the flashes, but Jordan still did all the original work. Naturally he took all the morbid ink jobs.

Three months before Jake's parole hearing, I began having a recurring nightmare in which I was a mother tearing through an airport looking for my child. I would screech and fall to my knees and grab security guards' arms and be tasered to the ground. I awoke to Bing Crosby II howling at the sight of me thrashing in my bed.

But that was at night. During the day, I prepared the apartment for him, scrubbing behind the refrigerator and dusting on top of the bookshelves. I bought new sheets and towels, both pale blue. I filled the apartment with plants because he always said that green was what he missed most about the outside. I practised making chicken-fried steak and spicy meatballs, his favourites. I got a beer-opener key chain for his new key and threw out all my period-stained underwear.

The night before the parole hearing I'd gone out late so I came into the grey room reeking of whiskey and pot. My lipstick and eyeliner were smudged and my hair was snarled into a wasp nest. I wore a lavender slip with a ripped plaid shirt—which I'd stolen from Jordan—over top. I answered questions in vague, dreamy language cribbed from my own poems. Jake glared at me, and his lawyer, a puffy red-headed man who had prepped me the week before, coughed loudly as I explained that Jake would be coming home "to a dreamscape of love and chaos and the impermanence of desire."

"What the fuck are you doing?" Jake hissed at me, his anger making me feel vindicated and self-righteous.

Straight to your room young man! I felt like saying.

"Be good, my baby. I love you so much," I said.

Amazingly, the parole board decided in his favour. He would be released in a week. The day I found out, Jordan and I shared three mid-afternoon pitchers at the Drunken Mermaid. He walked me to my apartment. Once we got there, we sat on the stoop and stared at the sky, a cloudless dusky plum. Fat white petals from a nearby magnolia tree floated to the ground. I leaned over and kissed Jordan on the cheek, then on the mouth. He kissed me back with surprising tenderness, cupping my face with both hands. After a few minutes of making out, I excused myself, got up and puked daintily in the rose bushes.

"Shit." Jordan was standing now. "What about Jake?"

"Jake the jailbird." I burped and reached for his fly. "Want to come inside?"

Gently pushing my hands away, he took a step back. "You're only doing this because you're nervous about Jake getting out."

"Does a Baby Ruth taste as sweet in a park as in a penitentiary?"

"I've never told you this but the reason I didn't go to the wedding is because I couldn't handle seeing the two of you—"

"Okay," I said, not wanting to hear anymore. "Okay. Okay. Good night."

The next morning I woke up with peanut shells in my sheets. I could barely move my jaw and I spat blood into the sink. I must have been grinding my teeth all night. Stanza was curled in my armpit and Bing Crosby II was lying on the floor beside my bed, his dumb inbred eyes liquid and needy. After all his nighttime concerts, he had lost his voice, his bark barely a rasp.

Two days before Jake's release I was taking care of the shop while Jordan drove to his latest girlfriend's house for some afternoon delight, or so he said; in truth, I was pretty sure he was avoiding me. I was talking on the phone to my mom who was advising me to take things slow with Jake, to be prepared for toenail clippings on the kitchen counter and wet towels on the floor.

"Check before you sit on the throne," she said. "I don't want you to fall in."

The chime on the door tinkled and a policeman entered. "I have to go, Mom."

"Can I help you, sir?" I said to the policeman after a few seconds had passed. He was wearing shorts, navy with yellow piping, and showing off his hairless legs. I wondered if he waxed them, which seemed likely given the luscious curly black hair on his head. He carried a white bicycle helmet under one arm. He had one of those inverted pyramid bodies—wide shoulders, tiny waist—that commonly belong to rowers or swimmers.

"Yes," he said. "I was hoping to get a tattoo."

Stepping out from behind the desk, I gestured toward the coffee table covered in binders full of designs. "These might interest you."

"I already know what I want."

He smelled strongly of Old Spice deodorant and mint toothpaste. How many people had he sent to the penitentiary over the years?

"Perfect," I said. "Do you have a sketch?"

He took a crumpled piece of paper out of his wallet and smoothed it on the desk. A crude rendition of a baobab tree, violent limbs shooting out of a black trunk. I could tell he'd drawn it himself.

"Beautiful," I said, knowing full well that I should stop right there and promise that my colleague, the true artist, would be back soon. "Where do you want it?"

"Right here," he said, patting himself on the back.

"Great. Take off your shirt and lie on this table. Would you like me to close the blinds? It's pretty sunny out there."

Silently, he reached into his pocket and produced a vial full of grey powder. Ashes. "I heard this is something you do. It's my mother. She loved Africa."

Part of me prayed that this was a sting operation, that I would be charged and sent away for a long, long time.

"Yes," I said, reaching for his mother. "We do that."

He didn't cuff or fine me. Instead he took off his shirt, then lay on the leather tattoo table. After shaving and sterilizing his back, I mixed a pinch of ashes with black ink, carbon with carbon. For the next hour, the room was abuzz with skin and dark ink and thick lines, bars becoming a trunk and roots becoming branches.

I started thinking about what type of relationship this man had with his mother, about what would make him want to stitch her into his skin. I imagined getting a tattoo with Jake's ashes. His fingerprints on each breast. I could even imagine getting a tattoo with Jordan's ashes. Something meta, like a tattoo of a tattoo needle. But as hard as I tried, I couldn't imagine getting a tattoo with my mother's ashes. What would be the point? She was already there, thousands of her, millions, each one locked in, pacing every cell in my body.

THE COPY EDITORS

The Copy Editors decided not to pay back their student loans. This decision wasn't motivated by lack of funds—though between them their bank statements didn't read above four hundred dollars and their combined Visa bills were triple that—no, it was a matter of principle. Who would pay someone who sent a letter that read, *Please be advised that your balance are outstanding*? Surely, the twins reasoned, such egregious subject-verb disagreement rendered any contract null and void.

They were celebrating their airtight logic on Ronnie's patio in Kensington Market. The patios had just opened across the city, as tentative and splendid as cherry blossoms on a branch. It wasn't warm, but people were acting as though it were—the boys in short-sleeved shirts, the girls in dresses. Sitting across from Mike, Will squeezed a lemon wedge. The mist clouded the beer in his long thin glass. Mike was a step ahead, a wrung lemon in his mouth serving as a smile, juice dribbling down his chin. Spread out before them were enough wedges to make four normal lemons or one and a half genetically modified ones.

It had been a productive day. Not only had they stroked out a glaring but previously undetected redundancy from their lives, they had also, in the early morning, spray-painted over the second L on the shop sign *Youthfull Flower Designs*, thereby ridding

Toronto streets of one more typographical error. Yesterday, from the grubby window of a westbound Dundas streetcar, Mike had spotted the sign's superfluous letter and jotted down its location. Today Will rattled the can and guided the nozzle into a curative curlicue. That's how they divided tasks: one detecting, the other correcting. The perfect copy-editing duo, each with his own strength. Mike could find a misspelling in a haystack; Will could spot a comma splice a mile away.

The benches around them filled and emptied with people, like the successive tides of immigrants—Jewish, Portuguese, Caribbean—who had surged through the area, opening stores and restaurants, painting houses, planting tomatoes, stuffing empanadas with chorizo and spinach. All the while they sat there drinking, talking only to each other and planning tomorrow's edit: a missing s on a make-your-own-wine establishment sign on Ossington that currently read, *Ferment on Premise*. Everything was hunky dory until the Cerebral Experimentalists, also known as the Cerebralists, showed up. Composed of two girls and three guys, the Cerebral Experimentalists were a group of poets who had all removed or damaged parts of their brains with the aim, according to their website, "2 disinterrupt the ruts of language and find nu wayz of no-ing."

The Copy Editors and the Cerebralists did not see eye-to-I.

"Who is that girl?" Mike asked.

"I've never seen her before," Will said.

The girl in question was sipping on a gin and tonic and nodding serenely at George, also known as Wernicke's Area. Like all the other Cerebralists, his name sprang from his lack. George was the most prominent member of the group. He gave poetic performances in bus stop shelters and graduate seminars. From afar, George looked as though he was speaking normally, but the twins knew that if they were closer they would hear a wilted clatter of nonsense. Why, the twins wondered, would he shove himself into linguistic solitary confinement?

Despite the lopsidedness of her smile, the girl didn't look like the others. Her clothes—a jean miniskirt and a white T-shirt— were too conventional and unless the wispy, chin-length strawberry blonde was a wig, she lacked the telltale head scar.

After the fourth missed payment, government officials informed the twins that they'd transferred their loans to a collection agency. Mike and Will decided to move. Having consulted Craigslist and ignored all ads with promises like "newlly-built basement apartment" or "emaculate, clean!" they found a cheap place in Chinatown. They slept in the living room and converted the single bedroom into a rarely used office, as not too many copy-editing contracts were coming their way.

"It's too bad we can't write Mandarin or Cantonese," Mike lamented one day as they walked back from the grocery store where they'd purchased obscenely cheap produce and witnessed a crab scuttling across one of the floors, its claws raised as though in surrender.

"Yes," Will agreed. "Imagine how many mistakes are going uncorrected every day!"

"Did you notice the Cerebralist girl peeking at us from behind the hot sauce pyramid?"

"Yes," Mike said. "I see her everywhere." Meaning he imagined lifting her jean miniskirt up to her waist and pulling her tiny panties off every night as he rubbed his way to sleep.

"Me too." Meaning her strawberry blonde hair grew from the branches of all the trees in his dreams.

"What do you think she wants from us? Do you think she's really a Cerebralist?"

"Can we be sure it isn't a coincidence?"

"Next time, I'm going to say something."

"How? She vanishes a second after we spot her."

"We'll figure something out." Mike extracted a cassava tuber from the bag and waggled it in front of his crotch. "Any idea how we cook this thing?"

Taffy light spilled through the sparsely leaved trees in Dufferin Grove. The twins were on their way to save their next victim.

"So," Mike said as he shoved his hands into his jeans, "we're agreed on Operation Unplug the Phone to Avoid Further Menacing Phone Calls from the Collection Agency."

"Agreed," Will said. "Hey, did you see the thing in *Now* about those dumbasses?"

"You mean the Cerebralists' reading series?"

"They quote Broca's Area and—"

"I read that. What was it again? *Absence make present absent speaker no natural absent reader present construct the self othernessed one.*"

"Classic."

Neither mentioned the picture of the Cerebralists that had accompanied the article, the girl's head poking out between Angular Gyrus's and Arcuate Fasciculus's shoulders.

Mike pointed at the arena. "Okay, right over here. Did you bring the whiteout stick?"

Nodding, Will touched the breast pocket of his jean jacket.

It would be at least another month before there would be ice on the arena, but the rules were already posted in white paint on a red board:

NO

- Tag
- Roughhousing
- Pushing people on chairs
- British

Mike kept watch while Will uncapped the whiteout and added an extra H to roughhousing and the word *Bulldog* after British. He was just perfecting a special flourish to the G when he felt a tap on his shoulder.

"I'm almost done."

"It was better before," a girl's voice whispered.

Will dropped the cap and by the time he'd retrieved it, Mike had run over to join them.

Despite all their speculations about what they would say to her given the chance, both of them just stared. She wore a white jean jacket and skinny black pants. A cigarette hung out of her mouth drawing attention to her bright purple lips, which clashed with her hair. Still no scar.

"It was better before you messed with it," she said. "Funnier, too. Besides maybe these guys really hate British people."

Waving smoke out of his face, Mike was the first to speak. "Doesn't fit with the context of the sign. All the other items refer to types of behaviour, not nationality."

"Killjoy," she said.

"Let me guess. You're going to spout some bullshit about the empty relationship between the signifier and the signified. Or about the multivalency of language."

"Now that you mention it." She ground the butt into the concrete with her Doc Marten.

"Listen," Will said. "That's just theory-head nonsense. We're on the front lines here, preserving the dignity of the English language."

"Who pays any attention to the syntax of things that will never wholly kiss you," she said.

Mike stepped in. "Now how about you tell us why you've been following us around?"

"Thought you'd never ask. You see, I'm doing my Ph.D. on the Cerebralists."

"Waste of time," Will said.

"Bet she's funded out her ass."

"As a matter of fact yes, I am indebted to the Social Sciences and Humanities Research Council, but that is neither here nor there. My Ph.D. on the Cerebralists needs a little more context, more conflict, and I'm hoping to include a chapter on you two. I've been watching your work for a while, and I think I'm ready to interview you now to flesh the whole thing out."

"When?" Will asked.

Mike glared at Will. "We're not interested."

"If you change your mind, here's my number." She handed both twins pieces of paper on which were written: Vanesa, one s, and her phone number. Then she walked over to her bike, which was leaning against the brick wall of the Dufferin Grove Centre. As she pedalled away, Vanesa yelled over her shoulder, "I'll pay you a thousand bucks each."

Mike sipped his bourbon and Sprite out of a jam jar and tried hard not to stare at Vanesa's ass, crammed into tight jeans, as she bent down to open her oven and retrieve a steaming sheet of chocolate chip cookies.

"Don't get too excited," she said. "They're Pillsbury, not home-made."

"Whatever," he said. "I'm kind of in a hurry."

Vanesa chiselled the cookies off the plate with a spatula and placed them in front of Mike on the kitchen table. *Click* went the tape recorder and down sat Vanesa across from him. "Please state your name and occupation."

"Mike Young. Copy editor."

"Good. Now Mike, could you give us a brief summary of your activities as a copy editor?"

"We fix any incorrect sign postings around Toronto."

"And why do you do this?"

Mike took a bite of a cookie and immediately regretted it as the chocolate heat scorched a layer off his tongue. "To bring orther to the world."

"Orther?"

"Sorry, the cookie is a bit hot. I meant order."

"Well, that's ambitious."

"It's an ambition worth having. It's an achievable ambition and an ethical one. Language used to be a noble stallion, but now people treat him like he's glue."

"He?"

"You're right. I should have said him or her. Gender bias is more Will's specialty."

"And you think that the Cerebralists are part of this corruption of language?"

"Absolutely. They try to reduce it to electric pathways in the brain, a cognitive blip. They abdicate their reason, their ability to control language to the whimsy of the brain. They're cognitive fatalists."

"And what would you say to someone considering joining them?"

"I would urge him or her not to."

Vanesa licked her finger, leaned over the table and rubbed a speck of chocolate off Mike's lips. "Would you urge me not to?"

Mike took a deep breath and closed his eyes and by the time he opened them Vanesa's shirt was off and he was staring at her breasts, smallish with loonie-sized nipples.

"Urge," he said.

"Yes," she said, pushing his chair back and straddling him.

The red light on the tape recorder stayed on.

On his way to Vanesa's, Will noticed a flyer taped to a tree:

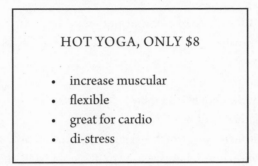

He didn't have the energy to fix the entire shoddy mess, but he turned the I in di-stress into an E. The correction was rote, pure habit. There hadn't been any joy in it since he and Mike started copy-editing the city alone. It happened one evening when the collection guy came around and started banging on the door.

Will peeked through the peephole and saw a repo guy standing there, muscles popping through his shirt. "Shit!"

"Ssssshhhhhhh, dumbass," whispered Mike.

"I heard you," the man said. "Don't make me call the police."

"Don't open it," Mike said, but Will had already unfastened the latch.

"I'll need that television," he pointed at the ancient black and white in the corner. "That computer. That couch. That bookcase."

"Wait a sec," Mike pleaded as the man yanked the *Strunk and White* off the shelf and tossed it on the floor.

"Here, would this make a difference?" Mike opened the *Chicago Manual of Style* and pulled out an envelope fat with bills and handed it to the man. The man stopped and counted the money before shoving it into his pocket.

"I never saw you," he said as he made his way out the door.

Once he was safely out of earshot, Mike said, "Well, I'd guess I better be honest with you. I did the interview."

"So did I," said Will. "How do you think we paid the last two months rent?"

"Wait, you did the interview, too? I am deeply hurt but I forgive you because you are my brother."

"I forgive you, too, but now that we're being honest, there's something more."

"Yes, I have something more to tell you, too."

"You first."

"No, you."

"I'm in love with her!"

"Well, I've been sleeping with her."

"Yes," said Will. "That's what I meant."

"Oh," Mike said.

The memory made Will pull his scarf on tighter. He was on his way to Vanesa's apartment, a tiny bachelor in Little Korea above a karaoke bar. On nights when he slept over he could hear soulful renditions of "Purple Rain" and "Life Is a Highway," the smell of alcohol practically seeping through the floorboards. Most of the time Will could forget about Mike, but once he found one of his undershirts draped over the back of a chair and another time, Vanesa called out Mike's name as she dug her fingernails into his back, rocking to climax. On these occasions, Will would joke bleakly with his inner Mike: *Well, at least she believes in parallel structure.*

Last time he'd seen Vanesa, she'd said, "I'm adopting a more experiential research methodology paradigm."

"You're being redundant," Will had said. "Is it methodology or paradigm?" He couldn't deal with the meaning behind her statement.

"Surgery is scheduled for next Saturday. Will you come and see me? Saturday afternoon?"

"Of course."

He pressed on the buzzer and, receiving no answer, tried the door. It was unlocked, so he let himself in, climbing the flight of stairs that led to her apartment. He could hear people talking, waves of jabber that grew louder and louder, but he couldn't make out the individual words. A champagne cork flew past his head as he entered the noise. The Cerebralists were guzzling champagne out of jars and measuring cups, huddled around the tape recorder at the kitchen table, hooting with laughter.

"It may sound idealistic, but I believe that we can strive, we must strive for transparency and clarity of language. Only then can we live in a just society." It was Will's voice.

No one seemed to notice him. He made his way towards Vanesa's bed. Mike was already there, holding her hand. Her beautiful hair lay in drifts on the floor. Bandages caked with blood were wound turban-tight around her head.

"You're here," Mike said.

"Yes," Will said.

"It's too late. She's totally out of it. The Cerebralists conked her out with some heavy-duty meds."

"What parts did they take out?"

"Corpus Callosum."

"The part that joins the left and the right side of the brain. What will that do?"

"No one will tell me."

By then the Cerebralists had reached the part of the tape where Will began to grunt toward orgasm.

"This is bullshit." Will stomped over to George and scraped the poet's chair away from the table. "What's going to happen to her?"

George launched into emphatic gobbledygook, punctuated by Will's moans. At the end of the sermon, he patted Will on the back and handed him an envelope. "Heshe got plink."

Red pounding in his face, Will raised his arm, setting off a fit of Cerebralist giggles, but Mike restrained him. "It's not worth it."

After absentmindedly pocketing the envelope, Will walked back toward Vanesa with Mike following. "I never understood her," Will said.

Mike put his arm around him.

Will continued, "Can one person love two people equally or does it have to mean two different things?"

"I don't know." Mike retracted his hold on his brother and moved to the other side of the bed.

"Do you think she loved us?" Will's hand grazed her bandages.

"I think she was loved by us."

As the Cerebralists babbled in the background, the twins kissed Vanesa on the cheeks, both at the same time.

Huddled at the bottom of the stairs, they opened the envelope. It was a letter from Student Loans stating that their loans had been paid off. There was a short letter attached.

> You wouldn't believe how much the university is paying me. Couldn't have gotten the fellowship money without my loyal subjects (objects?).
> Love,
> Vanessa

Silently they walked to Christie station. On the way, Mike stopped Will and pointed to a sign hung in the window of a beauty parlour.

> Magic Perm - $60
>
> Half Magic Perm - $30

"Does the half refer to the perm?"

"How can you halve magic?"

"Duh, aren't we the perfect example?"

"That makes no sense."

"Doesn't it?"

Without jotting down the location, they carried on.

OLIVIA AND CHRIS

Olivia's firm stomach rested on her thighs, her forehead pressed against the mat, palms turned upwards, poised to receive the universe's bounty. *Balasana,* child's pose. "Breathe," the instructor said, walking between the mats and exaggerating her own breath until it sounded like surf roaring against a rocky shore.

Olivia inhaled the rich, mossy scent of sandalwood essence and sweat—no, she corrected herself, *glow*. They were glowing, all of them.

"Breathe with intention as you push into downward dog." A month ago the instructor had advised Olivia to visualize her breath flowing out through the open window, coasting across Quebec, New Brunswick, Nova Scotia, cooling as it crossed the Atlantic and warming again as it gusted southward until finally it drifted through open lips and slid sweetly down an umbilical cord into her babies. Olivia tried but was distracted by the woman in front of her whose tattoo-garlanded arms shook with the exertion.

"Good job, mommies. Three more seconds."

Olivia attempted to ground herself with self-talk: *Through our yoga practice all of us are connecting to our unborn children who are growing strong in the wombs of the Gujarat women. All of us except for that woman whose ripe belly presses against her black top.*

Chris was the only one in the prenatal yoga class who was physically pregnant. But she didn't mind. She liked being the most extreme person in the room. That's what led her to become a surrogate in the first place. For Chris, surrogacy was a form of self-binding, a technique she'd read about in *Psychology Today* magazine. The idea was that people had multiple selves competing inside them, some of whom wanted destructive things, so when the good self was at the helm of the mind it made an executive decision to defy the other wayward selves. For example, the good self hid the video games in a weird place in the basement or it told its friends not to let it bum cigarettes no matter how much it begged. Or, in Chris's case, it decided to rent out its uterus to a baby, forcing the other selves to stop boozing.

At first Chris worked for a surrogacy agency, but they took too big a cut of her income, so she decided to work for herself. She hired someone to make her a website. Her profile picture showed her decked out in a housedress and frilly apron, red lips pulled into a campy smirk as she removed cinnamon buns from an oven. Within a week she was swamped with requests from the upwardly mobile. She was part of the local pregnancy movement, composed of Westerners who wanted to reduce their ecological footprints by using surrogacy services close to home. Local surrogates were more expensive than Indian and Guatemalan surrogates, but clients were willing to pay for the ethical capital, and to avoid travelling.

During the final meditation, the students all lay on their sticky mats while the instructor closed the blinds and played a remix of whale music, a series of grunts, moans and squeals buoyed by an electronic reggae beat.

"Take a moment to congratulate your body internally."

Chris's body took this advice literally and tooted its own horn. Luckily the sound of the fart blended into a humpback's screech, but the smell of rotting cabbage didn't have a corresponding subterfuge and many women scrunched their noses, some going so far as to pinch them and fan their hands back and forth across their faces, as the instructor continued.

"Imagine yourself back in the womb, safe and warm in the waters of the mother, life-giver."

More like gas-giver, Chris thought to herself. *These women should try actually being pregnant and see if they can stop themselves from breaking wind every two minutes.*

"I want you all to give yourselves a pat on the back when you leave the studio today." The instructor pressed the STOP button, cutting off a whale mid-Lamaze wheeze. "Good job. Namaste."

"Namaste," said everyone.

From her vantage point on the floor Chris could see all the pedicures and shapely calves headed for the change room. She was struggling to sit up when a hand shot into view.

"Let me," a woman said. The woman had curly, light brown hair cut into a bob and was wearing a turquoise sports bra and black shorts with matching turquoise racing stripes up the sides.

Chris accepted the hand. Amazed by the ease with which the woman was able to hoist her, she nearly fell forward but the woman in turquoise steadied her.

"Thanks," Chris said, wrapping her hands around her incubating belly.

"I'm Olivia." She extended her hand and Chris shook it.

"Chris."

Chris gulped down some water as she and Olivia headed over to the change room. She checked her phone and just as she suspected her inbox was crammed with text messages from Beth. "rem 2 take ur vitamin!" "drs appt on wed!" "hope u 2 r having a gr8 class!" Chris dutifully moved her thumbs around on the keypad. "thnks, see you wed!" The Blackberry, like the yoga class, was micromanaging disguised as a gift from Beth. The Blackberry was vintage and it cost a fortune every month. Most people could receive messages cognitively, but Chris had never had a system installed—one of the main reasons why she was so popular as a surrogate: lower risk of side effects.

"Let me guess," Olivia said as she peeled off her sports bra. "Your husband."

"No," Chris said, trying not to stare at Olivia's nipples, which were tiny, fawn-coloured and smooth unlike Chris's pink saucers fringed with coarse hairs that she didn't pluck, because why would she? "I'm a surrogate. It was the mom."

"How interesting." Off came the short shorts, revealing not a single hair down there, same as all the other women in the change room. "We would've loved to hire a local, but we didn't have enough…" Olivia rubbed her fingers together to indicate cash.

"Right. Cool." Chris turned to the wall and removed her tank top, surprised by her uncharacteristic modesty. What did this woman want? Normally none of the other women talked to her. While it was fine to hire a surrogate, it was still a tad unseemly to *be* a surrogate, and Chris wasn't about to let someone test out pseudo-tolerant views on her. "Let me guess," she said snidely. "Gujarat. Twins. One boy and one girl."

"Guilty!" Olivia said. "Boy, am I predictable or what?"

"Um, well…." Chris, still facing the wall with its lotus-flower mural, pulled on a pair of wrinkled linen pants. "Don't worry about it?"

Just why aren't I having my own baby? Olivia wondered, sipping on her matcha latte as she walked toward her loft apartment on King Street. No one with money gave birth anymore. Hadn't she read a study just recently proclaiming that only 1 percent of university-educated couples were having their own babies now? But it was a moot point. Not only was she over forty, but she'd also had her first microprocessor installed in her brain a decade and a half ago, and the early models, as well as many of the new ones, were known to cause infertility. It was in that first epidemic of infertility that maternity leaves had all but disappeared from benefit packages, though they'd been drying up well before then. Now most of the people who Olivia worked or socialized with got their twins from Indian surrogates and their live-in nannies from the Philippines.

The following week Beth drove Chris to class in her gleaming suv hybrid.

"You're so lucky," Beth said as she helped Chris step down from the enormous leather seat. "What I wouldn't give to be going to yoga instead of back to the office."

Chris knew this was bullshit. Beth loved being an investment banker; loved gripping the trapeze of the market as it swung ever more violently; loved the definitive clop of her pumps down Bay Street and the cleanliness of newly printed business cards; loved the briny taste of a dirty gin martini at the end of a long day; loved it all so fervently that Chris sometimes worried about the baby. Pregnancy was a crucial bonding time and what did it mean that most Western mothers never had this physical connection anymore? Would never feel their babies kick? But whenever Chris started thinking this way, she scolded herself. It was the damn hormones talking. No use getting maudlin over some imaginary connection.

Still, sometimes Chris couldn't conceal her annoyance with Beth. At the doctor's last week, Beth had gasped, a nauseated expression on her face, when she saw Chris's stomach, the bright red stretch marks streaking across her taut skin and the older ones that now glowed silver, all tangled in a mess of faded tiger lily and cherry blossom tattoos.

Chris cringed when she had to confront the images on her belly. They were images that were connected to a time in her life she felt so faraway from that it felt like someone else's life. As a teenager, she'd been straight edge—no intoxicants, no sex, no meat, no body modifications. She'd worn organic clothing and swigged green tea. Then at some point in college she'd become a raver, living the next few years with a glowstick in her mouth, a pacifier hung around her neck and a mind forever bursting with ecstasy. After this felt old, she'd become a punk—long after punk's initial heyday. It was during this phase that she'd gotten inked and acquired an affinity for Jägermeister and bourbon. She never mentioned the former substance problems to prospective clients, who would, she assumed, have balked self-righteously, though Chris suspected them all of being addicted to antidepressants, painkillers and anti-anxiety meds themselves.

"If you think my belly's gross," Chris said to Beth, "you won't stand a chance during delivery." It was funny, Chris realized, that in a way, pregnancy had returned her to her former teenage self. She was rigid about everything that went into or on her body. Sure, she wanted to control her negative impulses, but she also wanted to produce a superior product.

"I don't know what you mean," Beth said, staring blankly at the sonogram screen. "I think it's all so beautiful."

Half-lotused on her mat, Olivia tried to stop herself from glancing at the door but that only made it harder. Would Chris make an appearance today? Olivia had always looked forward to these yoga classes, a welcome break from her job as a human resources manager, but over the past week the anticipation had become so acute that she'd been forced to take Valium to fall asleep.

The instructor entered the room and Olivia's heart sank. "Good afternoon, mommies," she heard as she shut her eyes and pictured, for the millionth time that week, Chris's pudgy back, the tendrils of green ink curling down her shoulder blades.

When she opened her eyes she saw Chris hustling in, looking frazzled and huffing slightly. How far along was she? Olivia guessed that it was more or less the same as her surrogate in India. Olivia had received the latest ultrasound of the twins that morning. The clinic in Gujarat always used somewhat questionable music to accompany the rotating 3-D images (the sole criterion as far as Olivia could tell was the inclusion of the word *baby*) and today she'd listened to Britney Spears' "Hit Me Baby, One More Time" as she stared at the babies with their toes and elbows squashed into each other's ancient faces. Dutifully she'd sent the file to all her friends, who almost instantaneously posted responses about how much the little aliens—*precious darlings,* a voice within her admonished—looked like her.

The class was uneventful except that Chris sat out the sun salutations. How Olivia had yearned to stroke her hair and rub her stomach. After meditation Olivia again rushed to help Chris stand up.

Four years ago, after Chris had read the *Psychology Today* article but before she'd made up her mind to become a surrogate, Chris's parents had invited her over for a twenty-second birthday dinner at their house, just the three of them. Wine wasn't poured, but Chris came prepared and took frequent bathroom breaks to swig bourbon from a silver flask embossed with a circled A for anarchy. Post-"Happy Birthday," Chris sucked butter cream icing off a candle, the wick's sulfurous plume not yet fully extinguished. Her mother, a petite, bird-boned woman who barely crested five feet, grabbed the candle out of her mouth, so Chris grabbed another, but her mother removed that one, too. As a further precaution, her mother placed the deracinated candles on a plate at the other end of the table from Chris.

"Mom," Chris said.

"Are you going to cut the cake, precious?" her father intervened.

"Mom," Chris said, louder this time. "What was it like being pregnant?"

"It was wonderful." Her mother closed her eyes and smiled. "I finally got to take up some space in the world."

At the time Chris had found this response vaguely pathetic, but once she'd become a surrogate, she wished she'd pressed her mother for further explanation. *How could you possibly feel like a big shot with your head in the toilet? Didn't the attention freak you out, your body a topic of public speculation? Did your feet swell? Did you wince when the sonographer applied cold gel to your belly? Were you scared? Did you crave pickle juice and vanilla extract? Did you wake up feeling clean every morning, purified by a night of flying dreams and orgasms?*

Instead Chris pushed her chair back and made her way to the candles.

"Am I cutting the cake then?" her father said, the knife's blade already half-hidden in the white icing.

"But what you have to understand, honey," Chris's mother said as she watched Chris lick a candle, "is that in those days pregnancy was associated with motherhood. Nowadays people would stare, and not in a good way."

All through class, Chris had been aware of Olivia's bright blue eyes gawking at her, peering through her legs or over her shoulder as she expertly contorted her body through all the poses. *Maybe she's interested in hiring me for a third kid,* Chris thought. Then: *I bet she'll have the cutest babies, with springy hair like hers.* But even if Olivia did just want to hire Chris, it didn't explain her attentiveness, her hand held out to Chris before Chris even registered that she needed help getting up.

"I think you're leaking," Olivia told her back in the change room.

Chris looked down to see twin puddles darkening her shirt. "Damn. And I wore the extra thick sports bra, too."

"Is it breast milk?" Olivia's voice grew hushed.

"Yeah," Chris said. "What else?"

"What do you do with it?" Olivia asked as she stripped. Did Chris imagine the slight gyration of Olivia's hips as she pulled her shorts down?

"What?"

"Yeah, what do you do with it?"

"Oh." Chris took off her own shirt before realizing that she was exposing her stomach. "I sell it to the parents. If there's extra I'll sell some to other parents, too. Oh, and when they need it I sell some to this restaurant. Apparently breast milk ice cream is the next big thing. They pay out their ass for the stuff." Chris hadn't spoken this much to anyone, let alone a stranger, in ages. She lived by herself, she couldn't hang out with her old friends because they were always bombed and she only spoke to her family on special occasions.

"Which restaurants?" Olivia didn't look disgusted with Chris's stomach; in fact, Chris could only describe her expression as aroused, her tiny flower mouth slightly open and her gaze intent.

It was such a pleasantly foreign sensation to be stared at in this way that Chris opted to change right there in front of her, peeling off her bra, nipple hair be damned. She dabbed the thick milk away with her balled up tank top. "Have you heard of Anthony's?"

"No, I don't think so."

Chris extracted a different bra especially designed for lactating women from her bag, snapped it closed and pulled on the same black sweater, made of 100 percent natural fibres, as the week before. "I sold a couple litres to them last week. They're going to infuse it with vanilla beans or saffron or whatever, churn it into ice cream and sell it for thirty bucks a scoop. It's kind of silly, but yeah, it pays the bills, you know?"

"Wow, that's so interesting," Olivia said, buttoning up her navy blazer. "You live such an interesting life. I admire that."

The last gleaming button securely buttoned, suddenly Olivia seemed indistinguishable from all the other women who were busy clanging their lockers shut and turning their microprocessors back on, their eyes glazing over as they reviewed their messages. Once more, Chris felt like she'd been had. Here she was talking candidly about selling her breast milk to some high-powered woman. It was ridiculous. It was like a cow telling raunchy jokes to a farmer—no, the CEO of a dairy company—and allowing herself to believe that the CEO was laughing with the cow, not at her. For the first time in months, Chris craved the candied fizzle of a bourbon and Coke. She had to leave. Her compulsion for escape couldn't be slowed by politeness, and without saying goodbye, she booted it, her swinging gym bag nearly felling two ladies as she stormed out of the change room.

Not even Chris's abrupt exit could stifle Olivia's elation at having spoken to her for so long, listened to her husky voice, seen her stomach with its gorgeous tributaries of stretch marks. And of course, there had been the revelation about selling the breast milk. Although she'd pretended otherwise, Olivia did in fact know Anthony's very well. It was where her husband Michael had proposed over fifteen years ago, right after he'd been made partner. That was probably why he didn't find it suspicious when she suggested they go there that night.

When they arrived, the decor was slightly different than she remembered it. Gone was the exposed brick and in its place was a wall of moss, real or fake; Olivia couldn't tell, but either way it reminded her of a jungle, a lush orgy. How long had it been since she and Michael slept together? A month? Two? Before they were seated, the waiter asked them to turn off their microprocessors.

They shut their eyes and logged off—well, Olivia logged off but she suspected that her husband stayed online. Michael had aged so much in the past ten years but was still handsome, his skin leathery from tanning beds, his teeth bleached white and his body, like hers, controlled through a strict diet and exercise regimen.

"I'm not too hungry," Olivia said to Michael, trying her best not to betray her excitement. "Would three courses be enough?"

"What?" Michael said. "I'll be back in a sec."

Michael headed toward the washroom and Olivia scanned the room looking at the other couples in the restaurant: the younger ones leaned toward each other, the older ones laughed. She wondered how many of them had been deemed compatible by information their microprocessors had gathered on them—so much more accurate than those old Internet dating sites that relied on self-reported data—like she and Michael had all those years ago. Michael was gone for so long, or so it seemed to Olivia, that Olivia called the waiter over and ordered for both of them, pointing out random items on the menu. She slurped down half her oysters and glugged down a glass of Pinot Grigio by the time Michael came back. Without comment he tucked into his veal tataki.

"So," he said, "the big day is almost upon us."

"Yes," Olivia replied. In front of her, the waiter set down the second course. A quail stuffed with grapes and foie gras. "A month away."

"Olivia," Michael said, a speck of balsamic foam quivering on his lip. "We're leaving on Saturday."

"Right," she said. "Right."

"Sometimes," he said fondly, "I swear you're living in another world."

Somehow they made it through their scallops and devilled goose eggs, swilling wine as they went over the details of the trip, all the hotels and restaurants their friends had recommended to them. Finally the waiter came over. "Dessert for Madame et Monsieur?"

"No, just the bill." Michael took Olivia's hand in his and stroked it, his expression blurred, but whether by microprocessing, wine or love, Olivia couldn't tell.

"Wait," Olivia said as he walked away. "Ice cream. Do you have any ice cream?"

"Mais, oui," he said. "A house specialty. Breast milk ice cream infused with vanilla beans."

"One for me," she said.

"Very well."

"Do you really want that?" Michael whispered as the waiter walked away. "He said breast milk?"

"Oh," she said. "I think that's just the foodie way to describe normal milk."

"Right."

The ice cream was heavenly, creamy and rich yet simultaneously pure and light. It tasted like late afternoon sunlight. That night Olivia didn't brush her teeth because she wanted to taste the dense sweetness in her mouth as she made love to Michael.

Chris, sweating and red-faced, was trying to get up from the mat to ease the tightness in her lower back. Where was Olivia? She would surely have noticed Chris's discomfort and rushed to help, but the other women stared at her as she wheezed, an inelegant imitation of the instructor's explosive exhales.

"Push from your solar plexus," the instructor said. "It has to come from the fountain of power within you."

After much strain Chris managed to stand up, but almost slipped on the water that had poured down her legs and puddled at her feet. It was still too early, she thought to herself, but any residual doubt was squeezed away by the first wave of contractions.

Olivia came back from Gujarat with a jewelled turquoise sari, a sunburn and a pair of babies. There'd been no complications, and they'd given the surrogate a twenty-dollar tip, the standard amount according to the online discussion boards Olivia had consulted. Throughout the trip, Olivia had often thought about Chris, but when she got home she was too busy trying to love the new babies—it was still hard for Olivia to think of them as *her babies*—to do anything else.

The twins lay swaddled in their crib beneath a lacy canopy. Olivia's microprocessor collected pictures of them, which Olivia would sort through later, deleting the ones in which the babies were drooling or crying.

"I know an old lady who swallowed a fly," she sang in her breathy soprano, smoothing down the wrinkled sheets near the twins' toes. She noticed a yellowish patch of spit-up on the blanket and made a mental note to mention it to Bituin, the Filipino nanny. "I don't know why she swallowed that fly. I guess she'll die."

Following advice from her baby broker, Olivia spent at least three hours a day with the babies, even when it exhausted her. Purple crescents hung beneath her eyes, and twitches had taken up residence on the lower lids. "I know an old lady who swallowed a spider."

Just then, Michael appeared in the doorway. "What are you doing, darling?"

"Bonding with the babies," Olivia said. "Ever heard of it?"

"It's four a.m. The babies are sleeping. You'll wake them."

"I didn't have time today, so I'm doing it now. Three hours a day, or have you forgotten?" Her eyes back on the babies, she began singing, more shrilly than before, "That wriggled and jiggled and tickled inside her."

"Please don't do this. I have a meeting in the morning."

More quickly now. "She swallowed the spider to catch the fly. I don't know why she swallowed the fly!"

The sound of Michael's footsteps padding along the hallway was interrupted by a wail. Then quickly, a second wail. "Bituin!" Olivia yelled. "The babies need your help!"

Chris waited for her computer to load. It was already old, but she needed it to keep going for the next few years; it was getting harder and harder to buy hardware or software because just about everyone, not just the rich anymore, had wetware installed. Eventually, when she was ready to start a new life, she might be forced to capitulate and get a microprocessor. But not yet.

After the birth, Beth posted an enthusiastic review on her website. "Chris's services may seem pricey but they are worth every penny. I'm 100 percent satisfied with my new baby. She sleeps through the night and has a good appetite. Don't skimp on your progeny; call Chris today!" Ever since, emails from couples had been pouring in at an accelerated rate and Chris was having a hard time deciding who she wanted to work with: the older lesbian couple, both professors of law, or the young hip couple, he a graphic designer and she a PR specialist? And then she saw it. The name Olivia and the subject line: *need a hand?*

Olivia called in sick to the office and was now waiting for Chris at the Otter, a restaurant with large rough-hewn communal tables and blackboard walls covered in chalked murals of otter couples in Kama Sutra positions. Olivia had chosen the Otter based on a review in the weekly alternative paper. That the restaurant was attached to a hotel had been a bonus. She wore a tight, black turtleneck and slim-fitting jeans, the kind of outfit she would have worn when she was Chris's age. Watching Chris walk in, Olivia's heart nearly stopped. Chris was wearing a sage halter dress with the knot clumsily tied at her neck. The dress was tight against her flat stomach. Olivia closed her eyes and launched into self-talk: *You knew she wasn't pregnant anymore. She said so in the text. Push the disappointment away from your heart.* By the time she opened her eyes, Chris was sitting across from her.

"Should we get some wine?" Olivia blurted. "And it's great to see you. I'm so glad you came."

"No wine for me, thanks," Chris said.

Happiness gushed through Olivia. "Of course, silly me. You're pregnant again."

"Not yet," Chris said, a tight smile on her lips.

Her stomach may be flat now, Olivia's mind raced to provide assurances, *but remember the belly button pushing out, the tiny heart beating inside that swollen gourd. This woman is an earth mother, a goddess.* Olivia decided just to go for it. "But you're glowing as though you were," Olivia said.

The blush spreading across Chris's cheeks allowed Olivia to believe, for the first time, that Chris might truly reciprocate her feelings. "Okay," Chris said, her hands shaking. "One glass can't hurt."

A bottle later and the women were holding hands beneath the table. Olivia showed Chris some glossy photos of her babies—in all of them, the twins were giggling and Bituin, the nanny, had been cropped out. Chris talked about the pregnancy, told the story of her water breaking all over the yoga studio floor. It was this story that made Olivia propose they get a room, her treat. She didn't even care if Michael saw the bill.

Chris had convinced herself to meet up with Olivia because she was a potential new client but the second she'd seen Olivia sitting at that table, she knew she'd never believed that, not even for a second.

After tripping their way upstairs, Chris leaned on the wall while Olivia swiped the card into the slot and they stepped into the Sea Suite, a campy themed room painted bright blue with stylized seaweed stencilled on the walls and a bedside light shaped like a mermaid.

Chris fell backwards onto the bed, closing her eyes and savouring her first drunk in four years. She felt loose and buoyant. *But this isn't a step backward,* she told herself. *It's a step forward.*

This is love. I'm going to enter the relationship phase of my life.

"Is something wrong?" Olivia asked.

"No," Chris said. "I feel wonderful."

"Come here." Olivia pulled Chris up from the bed and kissed her long and hard, lightly biting her lower lip as she untied her dress from behind her neck.

It's really happening, Chris thought as Olivia kissed her face, then her neck, then her collarbone, then her breasts, then just above her ribs, then, then, then... Chris yearned for Olivia to continue her path, but Olivia rolled off the bed and was now pacing the room in her bra and panties, a matching turquoise set perfect for the marine theme of the room.

"Did I do something wrong?" Chris sat up.

"No." Olivia fiddled with the gauzy blue curtains, pulling them together then apart. "Don't be silly."

Of course, she doesn't want to kiss my awful gut, Chris thought. All those stretch marks gashed everywhere, the tacky swirl of tattoos so unlike Olivia's clean, smooth skin. Chris pulled a pillow over her stomach.

Olivia looked over at Chris, her eyes skimming the hump of blue concealing Chris's midriff. To Chris's relief Olivia crawled back into bed and laid her head on the pillow. Chris leaned back. The familiar feeling of pressure on her stomach offered even greater relief, though it hurt a little, too.

"I've got an idea," Olivia said. Through the dim light, Chris could still make out the whirlpool of plaster on the ceiling.

"What?" Chris's fingers were lost in Olivia's curly hair. "Anything."

"Let's pretend to be mothers." Olivia crossed her arms and closed her eyes. "You first."

DIFFICULT PEOPLE

These talks are mandatory, aimed at increasing our productivity. Last week I received an email from the organizer, Owen Peck. He promised "tactics to deal with Downers, Moochers, Whiners, Passive Aggressives and all other Energy Vampires in your lives!!" Sounds like Devon, I thought.

As I step into the boardroom, I take a moment to remind myself to smile, to participate but not in an overbearing way, to be cheerful not cloying, assertive not strident, to be a team player, and under no circumstances to mention Devon. Never ever bring up Devon. It's only after this bit of self-talk that I notice the mantra projected against the wall: *Happiness is the Power Cord of Success!*

Three months ago, on my weekly trip to my parents' house, I went downstairs to summon Devon. He lived in the basement, which he referred to as his Idea Incubator. Thirty, unemployed, addicted to energy drinks, aggressively curious, my brother spent most of his time writing and editing Wikipedia entries. He called my parents his patrons; it made the arrangement seem more reciprocal and dignified than it really was.

My feet, encased in nude pantyhose, swished against the cream carpeted steps.

"Time for another enfoodment!" I said, using our childhood slang for dinner. Well, his slang, really. Part of a faux-naturalist idiom Devon invented after years of watching nature documentaries (they were the only movies our parents deemed suitably educational). Devon could do a mean David Attenborough impression. When he was a teenager, his good days still outnumbering his bad, he used to give breathless, British play-by-plays of our family dinners: *What we have here is a typical Caucasian enfoodment. Notice how the younger female human does not bother to chew at all! The older male switches his fork from left to right and back again. Remarkable.*

That evening I was feeling silly and sentimental. I'd just received a promotion at work and was determined to maintain my sense of triumph, even in the face of my brother's inevitable disdain. He didn't believe you could be both employed and human. I called his name again.

No reply.

I decided I'd force him to laugh. "En-food-ment!" I repeated in a low, Cookie Monster grumble. Pausing before his open door, I rubbed my feet vigorously against the carpet, hoping to charge myself with static electricity.

Devon's room was shadowy, lit only by the monitor's bluish glow. Also emanating from his laptop was a faint pinging sound. As I got closer, I could see why: Devon's forehead was squashed against the keyboard, page after page filling with random letters.

If only I'd acted sooner. I couldn't speak or move. I just watched. Later the doctors and therapists told me there was nothing I could've done. If only I'd acted sooner. That it wasn't my fault, that he was already too far gone. If only I'd acted sooner. I couldn't help but blame myself. If only I had acted at all.

After a while I could tell it strained my parents and doctors to hear me relive the scene. They winced when they heard the word *if* drift out of my mouth. The worst part is that my brother would have listened to me, he would have been proud of how I let grief put my life together in a new way. But none of the living understood. Everyone considered it masochistic.

I wanted so badly for people to think I was a healthy, adjusted person—I have never been able to live far from others' approval. And so a month after a painkiller overdose scoured all life from my brother's body, I charged my Blackberry, responded to the 138 emails clogging my inbox and returned to my job at the bank.

Owen Peck looks like an ESPN broadcaster. Bald and thick-necked with a neat little salt and pepper goatee, he wears a blue suit, the blazer unbuttoned; his skinny red tie lolls down his white shirt like an anteater's tongue. Devon would have liked that analogy.

"Welcome," Owen says. "Welcome. Please take a seat."

Everyone is sitting in a circle on the ground. The men are mostly cross-legged. The women—all in skirts—have their legs tucked under or slightly off to one side. I resist the urge to skip around them, patting their heads: duck, duck, goose! No one moves to make room for me. Owen points between Marian and Roman. "Could you two scooch a bit?" Reluctantly they separate. *Do not take it personally*, I tell myself.

"Thanks," I say to Marian.

I plop down and cross my legs. I'm wearing pants. Ugly pants. Before Devon's death I would never have been caught in pants so ugly; I only bought them because they're made from a synthetic fabric that doesn't wrinkle.

"Decided to grace us with your presence," Marian says.

"If that's okay," I say, aiming for a meek tone.

Before my brother's death Marian had been my best friend. In the weeks after the overdose, she tried to help as much as she could. She attended the funeral in a black Chanel suit, obviously new, and kept reaching for my limp hand or offering me one of the bergamot-scented tissues crammed in her purse. She left encouraging messages on my machine and dropped off turkey casseroles with my doorman. Yet I couldn't will myself to accept or appreciate her kindness, goaded as I was by Devon's voice: *She probably read an about.com how-to guide for dealing with grieving friends. None of it comes from an honest inner compulsion, unmediated by society. It's all just repetitions of repetitions.* Naturally she began to resent my failure to return her calls, my coldness, and our friendship suffered.

If I tried harder, bought her a green tea latte and chatted with her about her pug Buster or invited her out for martinis after work, I could probably still repair the damage. But right now I'm just not up to it.

"Now, now, ladies," Roman says. "Don't be *difficile.*"

Over the years my brother contributed to thousands of Wikipedia entries, but those dearest to him dealt with famous recluses, hermits, eccentrics and naturalists. He distilled the lives and works of Thoreau, Julian of Norwich, Hanshan, Dickinson, Schopenhauer, Audubon. Right before he died he was working on a biography of Elmer Kleb, a Texas man who refused to leave his 119 acres of wilderness just outside Houston, despite hundreds of thousands of dollars in unpaid taxes. Oh, my brother loved these entries! He tended to them like a mourner at a graveside, excising additions (the factually inaccurate, the clumsily worded, the malicious), and laying down offerings freshly plucked from his research.

My brother subscribed to a Deletionist philosophy. The Deletionists are a group of Wikipedia editors who vow to uphold the most rigorous encyclopedic standards. Through message boards they debate the merits of articles, insist on the deletion of entries about people or ideas they deem to be poorly referenced, overtly biased or lacking in notability. This final category is especially contentious. Some of these online scuffles would sadden my brother for weeks. He never could convince his fellow Deletionists that Elmer Kleb merited an entry.

"It'll be easier once he's dead," my brother said morosely.

My brother would have been at home in a thirteenth-century

monastery, bent over a manuscript in a blister of candlelight, ennobling the words with his attention. His melancholy promoted from illness to calling.

Owen Peck gets us to introduce ourselves, then, pacing, launches into a speech: "When I say Energy Vampire, I'm not talking the sexy times kind of vampire. Don't get me wrong! I like a lady vampire in a corset as much as the next guy. No, when I say Energy Vampire, I'm talking a fat tick burying its fat face into your flesh. You know? I'm talking a slimy leech pumping blood like its leechy life depends on it, which I guess it does. But in this metaphor your blood isn't your blood. What is it?"

"Power?" Glen from accounting says.

"Close." Owen nods.

"Energy," Roman says.

"Exactly! It's your energy." Owen leaps into the air and does a little spin on the spot. He starts circling us, faster now. He is exhausting me. Everyone is whipping their heads to keep up, but I'm staring straight ahead, imagining the dense, grey cocoon of my duvet.

"Your zest. Your flow. Your primal spirit. And Energy Vampires are people who want to squeeze all that joy juice out of you. People who take, take, take. People who are just one long." Here, he stops and lets out an extended sigh.

The circle snickers. I try and fail to get Marian's attention. Is she buying into this?

"People who whine, complain, mooch, nag. Debbie Downers and Peter Passive Aggressives. You hear me?"

Everyone nods. So I do, too, even though this spiel is grating.

"People who never, ever seem to get the job done."

Owen stops in front of the projector. His shadow looms on the white wall, obscuring the mantra. "These are the people we need to exorcize from our lives."

My brother never managed to keep any job for long, not a job that paid anyway. My parents supported him. They were not people who could rid themselves of Downers. They tried once or twice, through threats or ultimatums, but one or the other would inevitably back down. After a while they accepted that he would never work.

Although he rarely expressed it, I knew my brother disapproved of my career. While I always made a point to ask about his Wikipedia entries and to feign interest in his responses, he never asked about my job. It was the elephant in the Incubator. Staggering now to think of it that way. My brother was dependent on my parents for survival, he had few friends and no girlfriend, as far as I know he was a virgin and yet by some strange logic I was made to feel like the pathetic one. When I was around him I often sensed the whole shining narrative of my life—business school, promotions, Liberty Village condo—snarl into a tarnished knot, worthy of nothing but scorn.

"Don't you think you should actually be contributing in some way?" he asked when I first told him about my decision to go to business school. "Instead of scavenging?"

"Why can't you just be happy for me?" I said, on the verge of tears.

He shook his head. "I think you could do better."

His disapproval was hard to take. As much as I desired his admiration, I needed the world's admiration more, and my young affluence was, I felt, the surest way to secure it.

As the session continues, I realize that Owen Peck is a kind of Deletionist himself, though my brother and his Wikipedia pals would surely abhor his criteria of notability. According to Owen Peck, we should surround ourselves exclusively with Energy Injectors, which he defines as people who have an infectious peppiness.

Beside me, Marian nods vigorously. *So there must be something to this,* I reason, *if Marian agrees with him.* I need to concentrate. *Be attentive not mocking.* Maybe Owen Peck can actually teach me something.

"People who think, how can I help this company? Who think, how can I improve myself and the people around me? How can I make someone's day? Those are the office cheerleaders!"

Owen Peck is describing the old me. The me who volunteered to take minutes at the meeting, to go on coffee runs, to come in early and stay late, to give up holidays, to cover people's work when they were sick or even just hungover; the me before Devon died and made everything pointless. *There you go again,* I admonish myself. *Be positive, be proactive. Try harder.*

As the afternoon wears on, he has us play a game of broken telephone. The original sentence, "I am not going to let anyone steal my life force," morphs into "I'm not gonna staple lettuce." I try to make eye contact with Marian as the group giggles, but she won't look at me.

The only way to coax my brother from his Idea Incubator was to suggest a nature walk. My mother, worried that Devon and I were drifting apart, sometimes called to suggest I take him out: *I know you're busy, honey, but a little vitamin D, some exercise, would do him good.* If he wasn't incubating some new entry, he always agreed. Without talking much we would stroll through the Don Valley Ravine or High Park. Last summer we drove down to Turkey Point Provincial Park, just the two of us, his—not my mother's—idea.

Ten minutes into our walk, a family stopped us and asked if we could take their picture. I agreed and twenty *say cheeses* later—they had wanted every possible configuration: father and son; mother, son and daughter; mother, father, daughter and chipmunk—they thanked me and ambled away.

I was expecting Devon to make fun of them, but instead he said, "You're so good with people. You have social grace. I've always admired that about you."

This compliment startled me. Couldn't he tell that it wasn't grace that compelled me, but a need to be liked? I mumbled, "Thanks."

"Too bad you don't get to use those skills much," he said. "Not in your line of work."

Of course, there was a loophole in the compliment.

"Get a load of that robin!" Devon pointed at a blue bird perched nearby; it jerked and cocked its head inquisitively before bursting into flight. An apt image now. My brother, a bird soaring. Me, a velvet-crested bulrush left wobbling after the hard takeoff.

"Okay, everyone," Owen said. "It's time to boogie. Everybody on your feet."

I stand and reach my hand out to Marian, but she pushes herself up on her own. My legs tingle and I slap them vigorously to get the feeling back.

"Role play!" Owen steps into the middle of the circle. "We need to work on some tactics to expel Energy Vampires from our lives. The best way to learn is to *do*. Volunteers?"

Marian grabs Roman's hand and raises them both.

"Great," Owen says as Roman glares at Marian. "A real power couple! Get in here."

When Marian advances into the ring, I notice how skinny she looks, almost haggard. Her silky peach blouse hangs slack and her cheekbones, exaggerated with blush, sharpen her already angular face. It reminds me, yet again, of Devon. Despite never exercising, he was always lanky. The draw cord on his favourite pair of sweatpants was always pulled as tight as possible, but it still couldn't keep them from falling down and he was perpetually yanking them back in place.

"Okay people," Owen says. "Here's how it's going to go down. These two folks are going to role-play. She..." Owen places his hand on Marian's shoulders. "...is playing the role of Energy Vampire, and he is the Vampire Slayer! We'll just let them freestyle for a couple minutes, then I'll cut them off and we can discuss what happened. Sound good?"

"Yes," everyone says in unison, with my "yes" trailing behind like a younger sibling trying to catch up.

Roman stands for a moment, dazed. "What should I say?"

Owen nods. "Maybe ask her something to get the scene rolling."

"Okay." Roman bites his lip, thinking. "Can you finish your section of the report by tomorrow? I want to get started on mine."

Marian slumps her shoulders and stares blankly at him. The circle titters.

"Did you hear me?" Roman sounds genuinely confused.

Cocking her head, Marian blinks at him. "Yeah."

"And?" Roman, now enjoying the attention, has shed his initial nervousness.

Marian sighs. "What's the point? No one will read it. It's all just shuffling jargon around. Might as well save some trees."

"Oh boy," Owen shouts. "Classic Pessimistic Patty."

"Marian," starts Roman, putting his hand on his heart, now really enjoying himself. "Your contribution is always valuable, but if you're saying you don't want to do your part then you should just be honest."

"I can do it," she says. "If it's that important to you. Personally I don't place much importance on outward symbols of productivity, but if you do..."

For the first time that afternoon, I smile. Devon and Marian only met once, and yet here she is doing a bang on rendition of him. Although I feel a twinge of sisterly indignation, I try my best to suppress it. I had forgotten how funny Marian could be.

"Nope," Roman says. "Stop right there. I won't let you drag me down into your negativity. I enjoy my job and I'm proud of myself, and I can't listen to one second more of your negativity."

"Great." Owen claps his hands. "Just awesome. Way to commit to your characters, guys!"

The actors return to their spots, and for the first time that day, Marian looks directly at me. A blush spreads blotchily across her collarbone, and she quickly averts her eyes. I might be imagining it, but she looks embarrassed. I'm filled with a surprisingly strong need to reassure her. While the others parse the Slayer's reactions to the Energy Vampire, I lean close. "You were hilarious," I whisper. "How's Buster these days?"

"Thanks." She forces a tight smile. "He had to be put down."

I place my hand on her shoulder. She glares at the ceiling, blinking back tears, and fidgets with her silver bracelet, tugging at a miniature martini charm embellished with a tiny emerald olive.

"Listen," she sighs. "I'm sorry if I got a little carried away."

I swallow and clench my fists, digesting the realization. Here I was starting to feel sorry for her, starting to think about renewing our friendship, and what was she doing? She was impersonating *me*. But I don't act like that, do I? *Be gracious*, I tell myself. *You deserve it after the way you treated her. Be understanding. Is everyone at the office laughing at me? Are they in on the joke? Be... oh, screw it! What would Devon do?*

I raise my hand. "I think Marian's character might be going through a tough time. She could feel misunderstood, and she might have some interesting new perspectives to offer. I think empathy would be a more appropriate solution than just cutting off all contact." Not quite as ballsy as Devon would be, but a start.

"Maybe," Marian says. "Marian's character could've explained that to Roman's character, and..."

Owen shakes his head as though we're grade two students who just guessed that one plus one equals three. "No, no, not Roman's problem. Marian's character shouldn't be burdening other people with her issues. There's no negotiating with an Energy Vampire. They'll never change."

"How reductive," I snap. "Surely human experience is more than that!"

"Looks like we have an Argumentative Andrea on our hands, people." Owen looks at everyone but me. They all laugh.

Breaking away from the circle, I head for the door. Maybe Marian will come after me and maybe she won't. It doesn't matter anymore. I'm exhausted. Before I leave, I yank the projector's power cord out of the wall. The room dims, but the eyes quickly adjust.

That night I settle down to my penance. The Deletionists probably won't let it last until sunrise, but at least it will be part of Wikipedia for a few hours. The keys clack reassuringly beneath my fingertips: "A typical Devon enfoodment consisted of a Red Bull and..."

MAJOR PRUDE

Carla and I wheezed through the same free Zumba class at the community centre on Wednesday afternoons. She couldn't follow instructions and was constantly cha-cha-cha-ing or grapevine-ing into me. Normally this would piss me off, but Carla's bouncy charm and gap-toothed grin prevented anyone from staying mad at her. Our ugly-sexy teacher Mario yipped encouragement and placed his hands on her hips, trying to get them to roll to the beat. Every week she got worse.

We bonded in the chlorine-stinking change room over our appendectomy scars and unemployment, and after class we started going for juice and then for coffee and then to the bar and then just straight to the liquor store. Turns out we both exercised to justify, or at least lessen the damage of, the too many beers and bourbons we sucked back. What a relief not to pretend I couldn't possibly have another! I could have another and another and another until I passed out. We would cut back soon, any day now. In September, maybe. After our thirtieth birthdays, for sure. Besides, it's not like we drank before two p.m.

Four beers deep into one of these post-Zumba binges, sunlight spilling through the condo windows, Carla told me about her smoothie man.

"He's the kind of guy who's never not on his way to a tantric sex workshop. He's never not comparing eating pussy to drinking kombucha. You know the type? Really boring about how sexually open he is. Going on and on about silicone, about Japanese erotica, about some bondage convention. I mean, it's fine, but sometimes it's a bit much at ten a.m. I guess his tactics worked though because he started getting into my head, you know? I'm sure that was the idea. He probably read about it on some discussion board. Say the word 'sex' over and over until the woman hears your voice while she's masturbating. And it's true I can get pretty horny the day after a bender. The world is all tenderized and porous, and I have this weird pinball of energy bouncing around my clit. Naturally, when I finally went for it, he turned out to be reserved and passive; a total bottom, and not an active one. Just lays there. You know the type? But every so often, it's nice. Plus, free wheatgrass shots."

I didn't know the type, but I laughed and nodded, like of course, totally typical. Men! Truth is I'd only had sex with two people in my life. Truth is it had been four years since the last time. Truth is I was kind of a major prude, the kind of major prude who needs to be plastered just to unclench enough to let someone insert. So I surprised myself by how much I liked hearing Carla talk to me this way, intimately, conspiratorially, as though we were both these carefree sluts slutting around town, trading sex for health food.

I stood up, padding along the thick white carpet—everything in the apartment was white or beige, too sterile for my tastes, but since I wasn't paying rent it wasn't my place to complain—and procured two more tall cans from the fridge. Carla opened my laptop and played some Dolly Parton, crooning and swaying along to "Jolene." She was skinnier than me and got drunk faster. I imagined grabbing her by the waist, imitating Mario, controlling her body so it moved to the slow rhythm. She really was a pathetic dancer.

The song ended. I felt dizzy so I sat down and gulped some beer, generic lager, none of that craft hangover-in-a-can stuff.

Carla scrolled through my music library and I heard the door scrape open. The only other person with a key was my roommate Liam, who also happened to be my stepbrother, but he never came home before ten p.m., and often didn't come home at all, spending the night at his girlfriend's instead. I yanked Carla's beer out of her hand and stashed both cans behind the beige leather couch.

"Angela," he said. "I thought you said you had an interview today."

"Tomorrow," I replied, though of course I'd blown it off. "Carla and I were just practising."

My stepbrother scowled.

Carla pranced over to him and offered her hand for a shake. "Do you want to practice, too? Let's role-play. What can you offer us that no one else can? Tell us about a time you dealt with an aggressive customer."

I blushed, assuming my stepbrother would realize we were drunk, but he smiled and shook her hand. Bewitched by Carla, like everyone else.

"Carla," I said, "This is *my stepbrother*." I hoped this revelation would temper her flirtation but it didn't seem to make a difference. She wiggled her hips.

"And what do you do, Carla?" he asked.

"Consultant."

"Consultant for what?"

She winked. "Performance enhancement."

Liam puffed out his chest. Did people actually fall for this stuff? She was practically fellating him right in front of me.

I retrieved my beer and handed Carla's back to her.

"Don't I get some?" he said to Carla. "I'm the one who worked hard all day."

She fetched one out of the fridge and we drank for the rest of the night, and when we ran out of beer, we went to a patio. Just one of those classic spring benders, blooms on all the trees and people in all the bars, newly recharged with vitamin D, letting their beast selves roam. Liam paid for pitcher after pitcher. I'm not sure if it was the booze or what, but he seemed looser than I'd ever seen him. He smiled, he cracked jokes, he forgot to lecture me about mutual funds. When he went to the washroom, Carla leaned so close I could smell her malt-laced breath.

"Isn't there anyone here you're into?" She pointed at various men, men with blue hair and gauged ears, men with glasses and punk T-shirts, men in white baseball caps with flat rims. Maybe I could approach one of them, fuck one of them, why not? Being around Carla made me feel powerful and hot but I didn't want Liam to see me hitting on guys. My face flushed and my throat dried out as I recalled how in high school he would snap my bra straps whenever they were visible beneath a spaghetti-string tank top. How I started wearing T-shirts, long-sleeve shirts, then thick sweaters.

In the morning I found Carla asleep on our couch, still in yesterday's outfit: a cropped tie-dye T-shirt and brown suede shorts with a tangled fringe hem. Liam handed me a plate of scrambled eggs flecked with green onions and told me he'd broken up with his girlfriend, which explained why he'd come out last night, but also presented some problems. Sure, he'd gotten drunk with us once, but that was an occasion tied to a breakup. I didn't want him to realize that being awake was enough of an occasion for me.

After Zumba class the next week, Carla bombarded me with questions about Liam. I deflected, told her he was a douchey finance bro, that she shouldn't waste her time on him. He only dated girls who wore Tiffany necklaces and had elaborate skin-care regimens

involving rosewater and glycolic acid. I admitted he could sometimes, on the rarest of occasions, be funny in a gross frat-boy kind
of way. I didn't get into our whole sad history. My mom's drinking.
Our parents' car accident. Liam ordering the lilies and delivering
the eulogy.

I was sick of talking about him. I wanted to go out just us girls.
Use those Zumba moves on the dance floor. Pick up guys. But
Carla kept pressuring me to text him. I said he had to work late, he
had a date, he was out of town, he was sick, all vomit and mucus.
Truth is I didn't want them to sleep together. She was *my* friend.
Plus, she was a little too fucked up for Liam. I was worried he'd
contract a disease or something, and he was vulnerable right now,
susceptible to her allure. The breakup had seriously messed with
his head. He was spending every night watching Bruce Lee movies
and stuffing his face with Cool Ranch Doritos instead of his usual
pseudo-Buddhist koan book and protein bar routine. He was too
lazy to berate me about my laziness. Eventually Carla stopped asking me about him. We still got drunk at her place instead, but the
energy was different—strained and awkward.

A few weeks later, standing in line at the liquor store, our calves
sore from jumping and our hair damp and smelling of melon—
Carla always borrowed my shampoo—Carla told me about her
latest escapade.

"There he was standing in the living room, in shorts and a neon
tank top. Thick, hipster beard, some horrible tattoo of Thomas
the Tank Engine or something spouting exhaust all over his arms.
He's holding onto my banged-up hula girl lamp. It's the middle of
the day, so I'm thinking he's on something. Meth? Molly? I don't
know. And he just puts the lamp down again. 'How much?' he
says, totally coherent, not fucked up sounding. 'It's not for sale,' I
say. 'I'll give you three hundred,' he says, and that's when I recognize him. He's the bartender from the Canary Factory! So I sell it

to him because I love that place, but then before I know it, we're going at it on the couch and his finger is in my…"

I cut her off. "Was he trying to steal it from you? Did he break into your apartment? Does he live in the building? I don't understand this story."

"I never leave my door locked. If all burglars are that hot, they can help themselves."

"Am I supposed to believe this actually happened?"

Carla pouted and we didn't talk for the rest of the wait time, just held our metal baskets and stared at an ad of a pixelated woman laughing and responsibly enjoying a single glass of Riesling. The silence expanded as we walked to Carla's apartment, a sad place in a squat, crumbling building. She didn't have the luxury of a stepbrother who footed the rent. The elevator stank of weed and grease and wet fur. When we got inside, I cracked a beer and rifled through the books piled on the floor, second-hand novels with disintegrating covers and layers of stickers gumming their spines. *Jane Eyre*, *The Bell Jar*, *Prozac Nation*. The same novels I'd loved when I used to read. As I drank, my heart softened. Did it really matter if Carla was pretending? Embellishing? Had I always been straightforward with her? Sure, we didn't have to hide our drinking from each other, but that didn't mean we were legitimately close, not like best friends in movies. I'd never told her about those fallow years of adolescence when I barely left the house or talked to anyone except Liam. Besides, I didn't want to go back to drinking alone, watching reruns of *Buffy the Vampire Slayer* and botching pedicures.

"Should I text Liam?" I said. "He should be home from work by now."

"If you want." Carla shrugged, barely concealing a smile.

Liam agreed to meet us at a nearby patio, the one with the wobbly wrought-iron tables and chili pepper lights. Mostly empty, it was just a few customers and some tattooed and scornful waiters. Once again, Liam played the gentleman, ordering drinks and nachos, refusing to let anyone else pay. "So," he said to Carla, pouring her another beer. "How do you help your clients improve their performance?"

"What?" Carla scrunched her forehead. She put her beer down on the rickety table, and the amber liquid sloshed. I steadied the glass, careful not to touch the fuchsia lipstick crescent on the rim.

Liam smiled. "You told me you were a performance enhancement consultant."

I poured my own beer. "She was joking." Under my breath, I added, "Not that I get the joke." I leaned between them to grab some of the chips drooping beneath an unholy sludge of guacamole, olives and cheddar.

"First," Carla's face was smooth now, and her voice deepened, like she was some late night sex advice show host. "I have to observe the client to see what their base level is."

He took a long sip of beer. "What if their base level is expert."

"Base level of what?" I said. "I can't track this simile. Metaphor. Analogy, whatever."

The two of them went on and on, ignoring me and flirting like two recently released inmates. I devoured the nachos, even the sad, dry, no-topping dregs and ordered a shot of Wild Turkey. I tried eavesdropping on other customers only to be bored by work colleagues lobbing acronyms back and forth. I tried to steer the conversation to Mario and Zumba, to novels, but nothing took. On my way back to the bar for another shot, I bumped into a muscular man in a pale yellow polo shirt.

"Sorry," I said, trying to angle around him to get the bartender's attention.

"Buy me a drink to make up for it," he said.

Ready to ignore him or tell him to fuck off, I faltered when he smiled at me with a mouth full of blindingly white teeth. I imagined describing him to Carla. *The kind of guy who spends a month's rent on laser whitening.*

"I'll let *you* buy *me* a drink," I said.

He laughed. We did a few shots together, and for some reason he started showing me pictures on his phone. The view of Lake Ontario from his condo window. Him in a shiny cobalt suit at some corporate gala.

The kind of guy who obsesses over pocket squares, who's a total square in bed.

He grabbed my waist and kissed me. I relaxed into it and draped my hands on his neck, pleased by the light stubble I found there—some gruffness beneath a sleek exterior. His arms were hard and warm. I felt protected. Attractive.

"I can call us a cab," he whispered.

"I need to go to the ladies first," I said, my heart bucking.

Under the fluorescent washroom lights, my face looked splotchy, my eyes red. Would he go down on me? I could feel my pubic hair growing, pressing against the weak elastic of my old grey underwear with the faded period stains at the crotch. Would he expect me to moan, to go on top? My left breast, slightly bigger than the right, swelled in its cup. Another time, I decided, when I could prepare myself. I sneaked out of the bar.

At three in the morning, I got a call. Carla crying, distraught, slurring her words. "He held my hands down. He was so strong. I didn't want to. Well, I did. But not then. I had my period. I wanted to wait. I thought, he's her stepbrother so he might be someone to wait for. Someone worth it. He's Angela's stepbrother. He's the kind of guy who might be worth waiting for. You know? You know? Your stepbrother is a fucking piece of shit. I'm sorry. I'm sorry. But he is. I'm allowed to say so. Maybe I'm a bit fucked up right now. But that's not a straight reason. Who knows? Maybe I led him on. He can't fucking handle his alcohol. Not like his sister.

Not like his baby sister."

Still blurry myself, I tried to ask her questions, but she rambled and rambled. After a few minutes I hung up and turned my phone to silent. She was too smashed. She didn't know what she was talking about. She'd be embarrassed in the morning. I went downstairs and drank everything I could find—beer, whiskey, crème de menthe, vermouth—anything to put me to sleep.

The next day I was frying an egg when Liam emerged from his room, yawning and stretching himself wide. *He held my hands down… he was too strong…* Carla's words kept cycling through my head. I didn't want to accuse him, but I needed more information. Carla was a liar, sure. But why lie about this? I was expecting one of her usual *Playboy*-style sex romp tales about how they did it in the washroom or in an alley or in a tree. Just a misunderstanding most likely. Too much booze. I wanted to hear him say it wasn't true.

He poured himself a glass of orange juice. "Your friend is a mess," he said.

"You're the one who boned her." The speed of my reply surprised me. And why did I use the word *bone*? I'd never referred to sex that way before. Maybe because it sounded cartoonish, like Fred Flintstone talking to the guys about Wilma. A bleached word. Clean and free of messy flesh. Much safer than other words I might have used.

He glared at me. "Is that what she told you? She threw herself at me, the little freak."

"You were flirting with her," I said, suddenly questioning myself. "I thought you liked her. Had a crush on her, whatever."

"Had a crush on her? I wouldn't stick my dick in that." He laughed, shaking his head as though he'd just heard a great joke.

"She said." I took a deep breath. "She said, she said—"

"It would probably come out covered in spiders and radio-active goo."

I nodded, uneasy. He was hungover, possibly even still tipsy. No point having this conversation now. I would press him later. Tomorrow, probably. In the next week, most likely. Sometime after he paid this month's rent, definitely.

I couldn't concentrate through Zumba class. I kept flinging out my right hand instead of my left, crumping when I should have been six-stepping and avoiding eye contact with Carla in the mirror. Mario winked at me and repeated the choreography in a louder voice. What would I say to her?

In the shower after class I squeezed a gob of orange shampoo into my palm and tried to pass her the bottle but she shook her head, opting to pump some thin, pink industrial stuff out of the free dispensers. She put her clothes on quickly so I had to rush, forgoing a bra to keep up. I held the door to the outside open for her and we walked a few blocks in silence, the brutal sunlight pounding our skin.

"I'm always afraid I'll pass gas when Mario makes us do those squats," I said.

She didn't reply.

"Beer store?" My voice sounded strangely hollow and high-pitched. "My treat. Me lady deserveth only the finest lagers. Oh, and I need to tell you about this dude..."

"You should really move out." She took a few deep breaths. "Your stepbrother isn't a good guy."

"He's a terrible drinker." I needed to deescalate the conversation. If I could get her to laugh, I told myself, the curse would be broken and our dynamic would be restored. We would be two sluts slutting around town, in control of our own bodies. "Not like us wizened alcoholics."

"Angela." Carla stopped. "You know it's more serious than that. I'm going to press charges."

"Do you really think the police would believe you?" What

the fuck was I talking about? I was scrambling. I hadn't expected the conversation to go this way, had expected more doubt, more room for alternate interpretations. Part of me was angered by her certainty. I'd always given Liam the benefit of the doubt, even when he walked in on me in the shower or when he left porn open on his laptop. It was a mistake, a guy thing. Why make such a big deal? "I don't want you to go through all that, put Liam through all that and for what? You're not exactly a virgin. He's an asshole, fine. It was bad sex, fine. But let's just leave it at that."

"I get that you're protecting yourself, Angela. I appreciate that you rely on him and everything." She stopped walking. "But you are being massively shitty right now."

"I'm not protecting myself. I'm protecting you! Wouldn't it be better to make this one of your stories? You know? Wouldn't it be easier? *I met this guy in my friend's living room. Total basic bro, always droning on about mutual funds, but he looked like my friend so I figured that could be an interesting twist on a tired genre.* That kind of thing?"

Carla whimpered. "Fuck you, Angela. Seriously." She walked ahead at a fast clip. I didn't try to catch up.

Every week I told myself I'd go back to Zumba and every week I talked myself out of it. I dialled her number and hung up after one ring. I imagined conversations with her, conversations in which I apologized with trembling eloquence and she punched me playfully on the arm and we laughed and laughed, maybe even went for beers, on me of course. Once I thought I saw her exiting a corner store and I ducked into an alleyway to avoid her, my hands shaking, my tongue parched. What could I have done? She got herself into these horrible situations. I missed her terribly. I told myself she was too far gone. She would drag me down with her. I only had enough energy to get my own shit together.

And I did get my shit together, sort of. I stopped drinking, mostly. Nothing is ever that clean, but overall my life became soberish. I got a job at a call centre out in the suburbs and worked my way up to manager. When Liam got married and moved to Vancouver, we stopped talking. No big confrontation, no recriminations, no confessions, just nothing left to say. That is, nothing I could bring myself to say. I moved into my own apartment, painted the walls purple and blue and filled it with ugly secondhand furniture with paisley upholstery. I started dating a guy I met on the Internet, a patient divorced dad who cooked carbonara and took me hiking. I learned what it felt like to have sex without being wasted. Pretty great, but also confusing and sometimes awkward and disappointing. I wished I could talk to Carla about it.

A decade after my last encounter with her, I was at a bland corporate pub eating lunch with call centre co-workers when I saw her sitting at the bar. I considered ignoring her, nodded distractedly while everyone else ate soggy onion rings and one-upped each other with tales of rude customers, but then I became worried she'd spotted me. Taking a deep breath, I walked over, hyperaware of my surroundings: my flats whacking the floor, the dust coating a sad plastic fern, a server squeezing chlorinated mist out of a nozzle and wiping the filthy table with a rag.

As I got nearer I could see Carla was drinking a can of Diet Coke through a straw and highlighting things in a textbook. Maybe she'd gotten sober, too. I fought the desire to lean in close enough to read the words she'd glazed in yellow. Was she studying nursing, accounting, psychology? Screwing my face into a smile, I tapped her shoulder. A muted cucumber smell rose from her hair. She swivelled the stool.

"Carla." Facing her head on, I could see that she'd gained weight, her cheeks looked plumper. She was wearing muted neutral makeup and no jewellery. Her grey cardigan strained at the buttons. Nodding distantly, she scanned the room over my shoulder as though looking for someone more interesting to talk to, as though planning her escape. I wondered if she was stoned or zonked on antidepressants.

"It's Angela. Haven't aged too well, I guess?" I said and forced a laugh.

She closed her eyes and massaged the bridge of her nose. "I know who you are."

"You look great," I said, floundering a bit, wanting to keep it light. I swayed along to the music, a teen love ballad swelling with auto-tuned emotion. "Still Zumba-ing? I don't have much time for exercise these days."

The veins on her forehead pulsed as she pinched her nose harder. Was she going to keep her eyes closed this whole time? At least I was attempting to reconcile, that was something, some small progress. It was stupid of me to think she would acknowledge me. I was nothing to her.

"Better get back to the grind," I said, though I'd never used that phrase before. "Nice to see you."

She opened her eyes. "Is this more what you had in mind, Angela?" she said, her words cold and severe. She bobbed her head from side to side, her ponytail whipping her neck more and more frantically as she spoke in a grotesque slurred voice. "Liam's the kind of guy who's never not waxing his chest hair. You know? Super corny in the sack. Wants me to call him Daddy, ordering me around. Obviously learned all his sex moves from porn movies and not the progressive ones either. Not feminist porn award-winners. Would have jizzed all over my face if I let him…"

I stood there, my knees unsteady and my face numb. I stood there, waves of shame passing over me. I stood there and listened.

THEM

I placed three live crickets and a teaspoon of vitamin powder in a Ziploc bag and shook it until the insects were coated white: a reptile's Shake 'n Bake. Lifting the lid of the terrarium, I airdropped the meal. Hera and Zeus didn't seem to notice the hyper ghosts hopping around them in a cloud of nutrient-enhanced dust. They lounged on driftwood, sunning themselves under the heat lamp like a retired couple comatose beneath the Florida sun. It was my fault. They'd been spoiled by the apricot baby food I gave them when I was too lazy to pick up crickets from Pets, Companions & Beyond.

It was nine p.m., half an hour until party time. My outfit had been selected days ago, but when I tried on the silver mini-dress again it seemed flashy. Instead I opted for a chambray button-down tucked into a maroon pencil skirt. I applied blush, eyeliner, mascara. The fuchsia lipstick was wiped off almost as soon as it was applied. Too brash.

I draped a sheet over the geckos' home.

"Nobody better mess with you tonight," I whispered.

The living room, recently tidied and vacuumed by me, contained a red sofa and several mismatched chairs that Taylor and I had found on people's lawns. There was a bookshelf along one wall and a coffee table in the centre of the room, on which I'd positioned a tasteful array of cheeses, crackers and olives. Now that we'd officially graduated, it was time to adult it up.

Taylor, my roommate and best friend, was holed up in her bedroom with her girlfriend Caroline. Again. It was Taylor's twenty-third birthday.

I knocked on her door. "Want a drink?"

Giggles and shushes.

"We're okey-doke in here," Taylor said.

Weed.

I poured myself a rye and ginger and fiddled with my playlist, a mix of songs that Taylor and I had loved as teenagers. Heavy on the Radiohead and the Alanis Morissette with a little Salt-N-Pepa thrown in. It was a pointless activity given that Caroline would almost certainly take over DJ duties, which meant we were in for a lot of Bikini Kill.

The doorbell rang and I went downstairs to answer it. A trio of girls wearing Doc Martens and jean jackets crowded inside. I didn't recognize any of them, so they were probably from the Centre.

"Taylor!" one of them yelled. Another screamed, "Happy birthday, bitch!"

More people arrived. Our mutual friends from high school, in various states of inebriation and bravado, heartbroken or broke or both. My friends from Teachers College with their loud voices and debt. Taylor's engineering friends, who would inevitably at some point in the evening try to convince me to play Strip Settlers of Catan. Everyone crammed into our small front hallway. The requisite shoe pile was in its infancy.

Once I'd herded the guests upstairs and directed them towards cups and ice, Taylor spilled out of her room. "Nice of you to show up," I said.

She looked glorious with her cropped curly hair and ripped Joy Division T-shirt. She wrapped herself around me. Her breasts must have been bound because her chest felt completely flat. This was a new development. "Kate, I miss you, babe!" she said in an ethereal voice that could only mean one thing.

"You dropped MDMA," I said.

"No duh," Caroline said, weaving around me toward a new group of partiers.

"Any extra?" I was trying not to sound needy.

"Shit." Taylor raised her hands to her heart in slow motion. "Did you want some?"

"Kind of." If Taylor and I dropped MDMA together, maybe we'd finally be able to talk. When we were younger, we talked constantly: on our way to school, between classes, after dinner. But I'd barely seen her in the last six months. When she wasn't diagnosing bridges or testing concrete—or whatever it was she did all day at her civil engineering internship—she was hanging out with Caroline or attending yet another workshop at the Centre.

"I'm such a jackass," Taylor said.

"It's cool." It was probably deluded, and definitely unhealthy to rely on chemicals to fix your problems. Even if it was easier. "I have to work tomorrow anyway."

Taylor stroked my long red hair, winding it around her finger. "I thought none of the boards were hiring. Wait, tomorrow's Saturday."

"It's at a tutoring place."

"Did you already tell me that? Shit, that's awesome. You get to use your degree."

"It's more like babysitting. I just watch them while they fill in worksheets. It's only thirteen an hour."

"It's something." She smiled dopily at me. "That's just great."

"I guess," I said. "How's the internship? Laying any bridges over troubled waters?"

She looked over my shoulder and waved. "One sec," she said, guiding me out of the way.

More and more people crowded into the apartment. The windows fogged. I replenished the cheeses and filled a new bowl of oil-slick olives plugged with pimento dildos. I tried to catch Taylor's eye but she was yell-talking about cantilevered bridges and queer theory to people I didn't know. My rye disappeared. The shoe pile became a wobbly cairn. Byron, a lanky blond dude and a fellow Teachers College graduate, handed me a plastic cup sloshing with red wine. I had the same three conversations—(1) we're never going to get teaching jobs, (2) this one time I was so wasted and (3) did you hear about so-and-so hooking up—over and over. When I caught a glimpse of myself in the mirror, I saw that my teeth had been replaced with purple witch's teeth. My lips were the scabby red surface of Mars.

I was in a we're-never-going-to-get-teaching-jobs bitchfest with Byron when Caroline tapped me on the shoulder. "Where's Taylor?" Her gold eyeliner was smudged and she'd lost one of her peacock feather earrings.

"I think she's in the kitchen," I said.

"They're in the kitchen."

I blinked. "What?"

"They're in the kitchen."

"Who is?"

"They. It's Taylor's pronoun."

"I didn't know that was a thing. She never told me."

"They. They never told you."

"Right, they." I was determined not to be an asshole.

"Okay." She smirked.

I knew I was only making things worse. "Taylor came out to me when she was thirteen, and I was, like, super supportive."

She shook her head in disbelief. "Great. I'm going to find them."

As I stood there trying to process what I'd heard, trying not to feel hurt that Taylor had kept another part of her life separate from me, a dim memory surfaced. I was very young, maybe five, and I was wearing my brother's hand-me-downs, sailboats on my blue shorts and a shark on my blue T-shirt, my hair cut short like my brother's, a frizzy mullet. I was running down the hallway at school, and a teacher was yelling, "Slow down, young man." I didn't slow down because I wasn't a young man and the floors were polished and slippery and I was revving up for a nice long glide. "I said slow down, young man." I could hear footsteps catching up to me. Her hand on my shoulder, the teacher spun me around. Searching my face, she released her grip, practically recoiling, anger draining out of her. "Sorry," she stammered. "From behind, I thought…" And from her embarrassed expression, her horror, I knew I should feel ashamed. Tears dribbled down my cheeks. A girl being mistaken for a boy, how humiliating. And when I went home, I begged my parents for something pink, begged to grow my hair past my shoulders.

Was I still that little girl desperate to be a girl or had I become the teacher? I didn't know, but I knew it was three a.m. and I was wasted. I knew I'd forgotten to bring out the birthday pecan pie, Taylor's traditional birthday treat. Too bad, so sad. Caroline should be in charge of that shit anyway. It wasn't my job anymore. I drank two glasses of water and slurred goodnight to the people I recognized. Two of the engineers were shirtless, and one of them was lovingly cradling a green wooden house in her hand. When I got to my bedroom, I found a trio gathered around the terrarium. They were tapping Morse code on the glass. The sheet was on the floor.

"Hey!" I yelled. "Stop that!"

"Chill," a woman with a shaved head and fake blue eyelashes said. "We're just trying to wake them up. We want to see them eat the crickets."

"Sorry," another girl said. She looked about fourteen with her black plastic bracelets, and striped pink and blue T-shirt. "Are we bothering them?"

"Are they Madagascar day geckos?" asked a balding man in a black hoodie. "I don't recognize these markings."

I shooed them out of the room and barricaded the door with my desk.

The next morning, after pushing snooze four times, I crawled out of bed and checked on the miniature Greek gods. Their animal instincts were intact! I couldn't see the crickets anywhere and this small triumph filled me with an extravagant optimism.

I changed into wool trousers and a grey v-neck sweater. I had to leave right away to get to the tutoring place on time. The desk proved a challenge to push aside. The alcohol must have given me super strength.

The apartment was trashed. Of course. There was slushy gunk all over the floor, and empties covered the kitchen counters and the coffee table in the living room. The remaining cheeses were smushed and there were olives lolling on the carpet. When I went into the washroom, I found the remains of the pecan pie on the toilet's water tank; a colony of cigarette butts stood upright in the dark amber filling.

I brushed my teeth and tried to scrape the wine film off my lips, but it didn't work. Fuchsia lipstick it was. I applied a thick coat and told myself I looked eighties in a good way. It took a few minutes to locate my jacket, scarf and gloves. I was all bundled up when Taylor materialized in front of me. She was wearing boxers and a white T-shirt, through which I could see her nipples. My cheeks felt hot and my throat dry as I recalled last night's conversation with Caroline. "Where are you going?" Taylor yawned.

"Work," I said.

"Work?"

I didn't have time to talk, but I also knew that I would spend the whole shift obsessing and re-obsessing and re-re-obsessing if I didn't say something. "By the way, I didn't know you were going by they these days." Did that come across as casually as I had intended? I wanted her to feel comfortable.

She looked surprised. "It's just something I'm trying out."

"Why didn't you tell me?" Not the tone I was going for.

"You don't have to use it. It's just for, like, people at the Centre."

"But I want to. I think it's so great." And I did think it was great, even if I didn't fully understand it. Not yet.

"Thanks." She was staring at the floor.

Even with all my winter gear on, I hugged her. I must have pinned her arms down by accident because she didn't really hug me back. As I pulled away, I noticed that I'd left a bright lipstick smear on her left cheek. It looked good on her. Them. They. Them. They.

Work did not go well. I was twenty minutes late and they put me in a group with three kids who all needed help with different subjects. One of them was francophone, and although I'd claimed fluency on my CV, that maybe wasn't 100 percent accurate. Who knew helping people fill in worksheets could be so challenging? It was no surprise when the director called me into the office at the end of the shift and suggested that I was not the best fit. For the first half of my bus ride home I spiralled into self-flagellation about my lack of responsibility, my ineptness as a teacher, my essential incompetence in the realm of basic human abilities, but after a while, I realized the tutoring company was to blame. They'd set me up to fail. Those kids were probably all ADHD or on the spectrum or dyslexic. And thirteen dollars an hour? Was that a joke? How could anyone feel self-worth for that wage?

I'd managed to more or less cheer myself up by the time I got home, but I still wanted an outside source to confirm my innocence and the vileness of for-profit educational institutes. I called out Taylor's name. No one answered. The place was immaculate, which was unexpected. Taylor hated cleaning. The swept floor shone, the couch cushions looked extra plump and the washroom smelled of bleach.

I dumped my stuff and went to check on the lizards. They were draping themselves regally on the wood like warriors relaxing after battle. It calmed me to see them so content. A creature vaulted from behind a plastic fern frond; the cricket was now marbled, grey with clots of white still clinging to thorax and antennae. Had they eaten one? No; the second cricket leaped off the water bottle like a diver off the high board. I considered punishing the geckos for their lack of ambition. If they had no other food, they'd have to hunt eventually, but in the end, I caved. I mixed some vitamin powder with the apricot baby food and put it in the terrarium. No reason why all creatures great and small had to feel like shit.

A month after being fired I got a job at La Senza, a lingerie store at the mall. It was a fluke, the result of an indiscriminate blitz of applications. No point looking for a teaching job until summer. Now I spent my days surrounded by leopard-print thongs and pink, furry handcuffs, the air thick with glittery vanilla body spray. Teenage girls bought G-strings in bulk. Teenage boys fondled the gel-filled bras embellished with rhinestones. A woman in her seventies came in one afternoon looking for shamrock nipple tassels. She explained that she only had sex with her husband twice a year, on his birthday and on Saint Patrick's Day, so she wanted to make it count.

If I hadn't felt low-level shame about the position, it could have been decent. I had very little responsibility and I could come in hungover with zero repercussions: a good thing considering how much I'd been drinking. With university buddies. With co-workers. With high school friends. But never with Taylor. She was a ghost haunting the apartment, showing up erratically with Caroline in tow to pack a bag before heading off to some retreat at the Centre. The last time I saw her she had a patch of mousy down above her lip. I wanted to ask about hormones and to reassure Taylor that even though some people might judge her for not adhering to conventional standards of gender or for marring their gorgeous face, I was not one of them.

On a Friday night in June I went out for goodbye drinks with Byron. He was moving to Abu Dhabi to work as a science teacher at an international high school.

"You should consider it," he said. "They're paying for my flight. My rent. Everything."

I helped myself to more amber beer from the pitcher. "Something will open up here."

"Are you even applying?"

I resented the implication that I'd given up. Mostly because it was true.

"Seriously," he said. "Do you want to spend the rest of your life working at La Sadness?"

"At least I get a discount." I winked. "Besides my babies need me." The Olympian couple had remained on a steady diet of Gerber. They couldn't possibly fend for themselves.

He rolled his eyes and I changed the subject to our common friends' recent drunken escapades and/or hookups. The conversation had made me a little manic and my drinking pace was more frenzied than usual, so I agreed when some of Byron's friends suggested heading to a club. I was wearing a sweatshirt and slightly saggy jeans, but I figured some eyeliner would be sufficient to glam myself up.

An hour later I was bobbing along to an electro version of "Smells Like Teen Spirit" and taking sips of my glowing gin and tonic when someone tapped me on the shoulder.

"Thought so," a girl with a shaved head said loudly.

I scowled.

"Tracy." She held out her hand. "From the party. You're the lizard lady."

I nodded, vaguely remembering kicking her out of my room.

"You're friends with Taylor."

"Best friends," I said. "And roommates. Since we were seven. Friends since seven, not roommates."

She laughed. "You might be even cuter than them."

"Are you from," I used air quotes, "the Centre?"

Then, somehow, we were making out. It was weird, but also kind of great. It had been months since I'd kissed anyone, which suddenly struck me as absurd. I was young and in my prime. I should be out kissing everybody. Hell, I should be fucking everybody. I'd only ever kissed one other girl before. And that was Taylor when we were thirteen after we'd drunk a bottle of Malibu mixed with orange crush. Did that even count?

Two days later I ran into Taylor at the apartment. She was sitting on the couch eating crackers and hummus and reading a comic book. She was wearing a denim shirt with a red bow tie. Their moustache had filled in. I forced myself to give a non-committal nod and then went to my room. Taylor knocked on the door.

"Come in," I said, arranging myself in a relaxed-looking pose on the bed.

She stood in the doorway. "Did you make out with Tracy?"

"Yup." I grabbed a four-month-old *Vanity Fair* off my side table and flipped through it, stale perfume rising off the pages.

"She asked for your number. Should I give it to her?"

"Sure." I really, really didn't want her to give Tracy my number. I'd enjoyed kissing Tracy, but it was more a starved-for-human-contact thing than a sexual-attraction thing. But I wasn't about to tell Taylor that.

"Since when are you into girls?"

I put the magazine down and looked her in the eye. "Since when do you give a shit?"

She walked further into the room. "Where is that coming from?"

"I haven't seen you in months." I sat up straighter. "Just cause I'm not genderqueer or whatever suddenly I'm too uncool to hang out with."

I'd gone too far. I could see it in her clenched jaw, in the red splotches travelling up her neck.

"That's bullshit," Taylor said with quiet ferocity. "Total fucking bullshit."

"Is it?"

"Thanks for the support," Taylor said sarcastically. "It's such a blast with everyone staring at me in public washrooms, with cashiers squinting at my ID. Maybe I don't want to talk to *you* about that stuff, consider that?"

"Why not?"

"It's awkward. You're so weird about it. Plus, you're always drunk or hungover."

"I'm trying." My lower lip shook, and I blinked hard, trying to stop myself from crying.

"I didn't wake up one day and decide," Taylor said.

"How long have you felt this way?"

"I don't know. Since puberty? Maybe forever." Taylor's voice trembled. "I want to see myself in the mirror. I want to live my life."

"Without me?"

They shrugged, pulling at a loose white thread on their sleeve. "I don't know."

We stayed there for a while, in that silence, on that crumbling bridge. I wanted to be happy for Taylor, supportive. I could see they were in pain, so why was I being so awful?

"I can try harder," I whispered.

Taylor looked at me, their eyes red. "I'm not saying it's all your fault."

"It's implied."

"I still want to be friends."

"Aren't we?"

"Of course."

"Can I ask you something?" I said, unable to stop myself now that we were talking again, now that Taylor had used the word *friend*.

"Depends."

"Are you taking hormones?"

"Perfect example of you being awkward and weird." They smiled and shook their head, curls bouncing.

"But the..." I rubbed above my lip.

They laughed, a big belly laugh. "All natural, baby. I just stopped waxing. Remember how you used to rip it off for me in high school because I was too much of a pussy?"

I remembered the hot resiny smell of the wax and Taylor's parents' bathroom with its mallard duck motif—duck wallpaper, duck soap-dispenser. The cold tiles beneath us as we sat cross-legged and I slabbed the wax on thick. How proud I felt when I got a nice clean yank, the skin underneath smooth and hairless.

"You used to squeal," I said. "Like a cat possessed by Janis Joplin's ghost."

"Fart face." Taylor punched me. "Scoot over. I'm cold."

I massaged my bicep. "So we're good, then?"

"Getting there," they said.

Taylor climbed into bed, pulling the floral duvet up to our chins. For the first time in a year I felt comfortable again. We talked and reminisced and laughed. I asked about their internship, their co-workers. They were all excited about a new form of bio-concrete, something about magical limestone-creating bacteria that were activated by the rain and could seal any cracks or fractures in the concrete on their own.

"So the concrete is alive?"

"In a way," Taylor said. "It can heal itself."

They asked about La Senza, and I told my worst stories in my most charming style, doing the voices, drawing out the punchlines. We gossiped about our mutual friend's terrible boyfriend and their terrible couple tattoos: a heart-shaped lock for her, a steampunk key for him.

"So heteronormative," I said. "Am I right?"

Taylor rolled their eyes.

I was feeling so generous I even asked about Caroline.

"Actually," Taylor winced. "That's something I wanted to talk to you about."

"Is something wrong?" I said with maybe a smidge too much enthusiasm.

"We're moving in together."

Of course. Why else would Taylor be so nice to me? They wanted me to move out of the apartment. The apartment I'd found. I was so pathetic I'd forgiven them right away. Taylor didn't care about me.

"I have big news, too," I said. "I'm moving to Abu Dhabi in the fall. Got a teaching gig there." What the hell was wrong with me?

Taylor clapped and drew me into a hug. I was surrounded by the sweet punch of stale weed. "I'm so happy for you. That's just wonderful! And Car and I can keep the apartment. I was so worried about finding a new place."

"Awesome," I said in a freaky high-pitched voice. "I'll be out of here by mid-August."

It was disturbingly easy to secure a job in Abu Dhabi through Byron's agency. All they needed was a headshot and a copy of my teaching degree. Once I signed the papers I found myself getting excited. Why hadn't I listened to Byron before? I stayed up late reading about the region and planning fantasy trips to nearby countries. Instead of hitting the bar after work, I went to Arabic classes. I decided to wean my geckos off baby food. It had been a week since they'd gotten any. Two crickets had died in their terrarium, and their corpses were still there, but I'd seen the leg of a third one poking out of Hera's mouth. The lizards were going to live with my parents. I had made them promise that I could Skype with the divine couple at least once a week.

My flight was in three days and most of my room had been packed for storage. While I was taping a box of shoes shut, Taylor called from the other room.

"Anything I can help with? I'm heading to the Centre's five-year anniversary party in ten."

"Nope," I said. Caroline's stuff had already started to fill up the apartment. Her fancy knife block was in the kitchen and she'd hung a portrait of Patti Smith on one of the walls in the living room. I'd been so focused on my own shit that it didn't bother me. At least not as much as it once would have.

I was going to my parents' house for dinner, but I had to feed Zeus and Hera before I left. They'd definitely gotten leaner in the past few days. I did the whole cricket/vitamin/Ziploc routine and opened the lid of the terrarium. Maybe I opened it too wide. Maybe they were just feeling more adventurous or more desperate. Whatever the reason, Hera darted out of the terrarium and manifested on the wall, then on the ceiling, then on the curtain. I slammed the lid down before Zeus could get out, too. I yelped. I shook the curtain and got down on my knees. Where had Hera gone? Taylor rushed into the room.

"You okay?"

"Hera escaped," I said. "We need to secure the area."

Without comment Taylor closed the door, and I stuffed my pink terry cloth robe under the gap.

"There," Taylor pointed at my bedside table. By the time I looked over it was gone.

"Are they both out?" Taylor asked.

Inside the terrarium, Zeus was blinking at the cricket, his tongue darting in and out of his mouth.

"Just Hera."

The gecko kept emerging and disappearing. She was on a lamp-shade. The door frame. A pillow. The speed of these apparitions made it seem as though she was travelling in and out of dimensions or being teleported. I'd armed Taylor and myself with empty Ziplocs to trap her. We were stalking so intently, with so many thrilling near-captures, that I didn't notice how much time had passed. Glancing at the clock, I saw that it had been nearly an hour.

"You're late," I said. "For your thing at the Centre."

Taylor dove under the bed. "Got her!"

They re-emerged with the reptile in the bag.

I twirled around and kissed Taylor on the cheek. Carefully we opened the terrarium and deposited the captive. It wasn't until Hera had landed that we noticed.

"Shit!" Taylor said. They dropped the bag to the floor. There was a slip of green inside, still squirming. A tail.

The sight of the truncated god was so depressing it was hilarious. I grabbed the bag from Taylor, extracted the tail and flourished it like a limp fencing foil.

"The poor thing," Taylor whispered.

Holding the bright green appendage at the small of my back, I wiggled my butt. "Can I pull this off?"

They smiled weakly. "I feel terrible."

"It's my fault, all of it," I squeezed their hand. "And don't worry, it'll grow back."

"It will?"

"I think so," I said. "It might take awhile."

Taylor, all flushed, held my hand a moment longer, then let go.

NOTES AND ACKNOWLEDGEMENTS

Earlier versions of these stories appeared in *Event, Joyland, Grain, Dragnet* and *TOK 7: Writing the New Toronto*. Thank you to the editors.

I am grateful to the Toronto Arts Council and the Ontario Arts Council for their financial assistance. Thank you to Emma Dolan for the beautiful cover design (and for her many years of friendship!) and to Amber McMillan for the insightful edits. Thank you to Nathaniel G. Moore, Silas White and Carleton Wilson for their belief in this book and their ongoing support.

Thank you to my teachers: Jeff Parker, Robert McGill, Barbara Gowdy, R.O. Kwon, Nino Ricci and Jade Sharma. Thank you to all the writers (there are too many to list!) who have read and commented on these stories. Your generosity and insight have made me a better writer and person.

Thank you to all my wonderful friends and family members. I am blessed to have you in my life.

And finally, thank you to Ted Nolan, who listened to me complain and doubt myself throughout the writing of this book. You always knew when I needed encouragement and when I needed to be left alone. Thank you for loving a difficult person.

PHOTO CREDIT: Emma Dolan

ABOUT THE AUTHOR

Catriona Wright is the author of the poetry collection *Table Manners* (Véhicule Press, 2017). Her short stories have appeared in *Geist, The New Quarterly, Grain, Event* and *Joyland*. She lives in Toronto, Ontario.